RBL

PENGUIN BOOKS

MY HOUSE IN UMBRIA

William Trevor was born in Mitchelstown, County Cork, in 1928, and spent his childhood in provincial Ireland. He attended a number of Irish schools and Trinity College, Dublin. He is a member of the Irish Academy of Letters.

Among his books are *Two Lives* (1991), comprised of the novellas *Reading Turgenev*, shortlisted for the Booker Prize, and *My House in Umbria*; eight volumes of stories that were brought together in *The Collected Stories* (1992), chosen by *The New York Times* as one of the best books of the year; *Felicia's Journey* (1994), winner of the Whitbread Book of the Year Award and the *Sunday Express* Prize, and made into a motion picture; *After Rain* (1996), selected by the editors of *The New York Times Book Review* as one of the eight best books of the year; and *Death in Summer* (1998), a *New York Times* bestseller and Notable Book. His latest collection of stories is *The Hill Bachelors* (2000). Many of his stories have appeared in *The New Yorker* and other magazines. His most recent novel, *The Story of Lucy Gault* (2002), was nominated for the Man Booker Prize. In 1977, William Trevor was named honorary Commander of the British Empire in recognition of his services to literature. In 1996, he received a Lannan Literary Award for Fiction. He lives in Devon, England.

To access Great Books Foundation Discussion Guides online, visit our Web site at www.penguin.com or the foundation Web site at www.greatbooks.org

William Trevor

My House in Umbria

PENGUIN BOOKS

PENGUIN BOOKS

Published by the Penguin Group
Penguin Putnam Inc., 375 Hudson Street,
New York, New York 10014, U.S.A.
Penguin Books Ltd, 80 Strand, London WC2R 0RL, England
Penguin Books Australia Ltd, 250 Camberwell Road,
Camberwell, Victoria 3124, Australia
Penguin Books Canada Ltd, 10 Alcorn Avenue,
Toronto, Ontario, Canada M4V 3B2
Penguin Books India (P) Ltd, 11 Community Centre,
Panchsheel Park, New Delhi – 110 017, India
Penguin Books (N.Z.) Ltd, Cnr Rosedale and Airborne Roads,
Albany, Auckland, New Zealand
Penguin Books (South Africa) (Pty) Ltd, 24 Sturdee Avenue,
Rosebank, Johannesburg 2196, South Africa

Penguin Books Ltd, Registered Offices:
Harmondsworth, Middlesex, England

First published in Great Britain in the volume titled *Two Lives: Reading Turgenev* and *My House in Umbria* by Penguin Books Ltd 1991
First published in the United States of America by Viking Penguin,
a division of Penguin Books USA Inc 1991
Published in Penguin Books (U.K. and U.S.A.) 1992
My House in Umbria published in Penguin Books 2003

1 3 5 7 9 10 8 6 4 2

Copyright © William Trevor, 1991
All rights reserved

LIBRARY OF CONGRESS CATALOGING IN PUBLICATION DATA
Trevor, William, 1928–
My house in Umbria / William Trevor.
p. cm.
ISBN 0 14 20.0365 4
1. Victims of terrorism—Fiction. 2. Women novelists—Fiction.
3. Ex-prostitutes—Fiction. 4. Umbria (Italy)—Fiction. I. Title.
PR6070.R4M925 2003
823'.914—dc21 2003043363

Printed in the United States of America

Except in the United States of America, this book is sold subject to the condition that it shall not, by way of trade or otherwise, be lent, re-sold, hired out, or otherwise circulated without the publisher's prior consent in any form of binding or cover other than that in which it is published and without a similar condition including this condition being imposed on the subsequent purchaser.

The scanning, uploading and distribution of this book via the Internet or via any other means without the permission of the publisher is illegal and punishable by law. Please purchase only authorized electronic editions, and do not participate in or encourage electronic piracy of copyrighted materials. Your support of the author's rights is appreciated.

My House in Umbria

1

It is not easy to introduce myself. Gloria Grey, Janine Ann Johns, Cora Lamore: there is a choice, and there have been other names as well. Names hardly matter, I think; it is perhaps enough to say I like Emily Delahunty best. 'Mrs Delahunty,' people say, although strictly speaking I have never been married. I am offered the title out of respect to a woman of my appearance and my years; and Quinty – who addresses me more than anyone else – once said when I questioned him on the issue: '"Miss Delahunty" doesn't suit you.'

I make no bones about it, I am not a woman of the world; I am not an educated woman; what I know I have taught myself. Rumour and speculation – even downright lies – have abounded since I was sixteen years old. In any person's life that side of things is unavoidable, but I believe I have suffered more than most, and take this opportunity to set the record straight. Firstly, my presence on the S.S. *Hamburg* in my less affluent days was as a stewardess, nothing more. Secondly, it is a mischievous fabrication that at the time of the Oleander Avenue scandal I accepted money in return for silence. Thirdly, Mrs Chubbs was dead, indeed already buried, before I met her husband. On the other hand I do not deny that men have offered me gifts, probably all of which I have accepted. Nor do I deny that my years in Africa are marked, in my memory, with personal regret. Unhappiness breeds confusion and misunderstanding. I was far from happy in Ombubu, at the Café Rose.

In the summer of which I now write I had reached my fifty-sixth year – a woman carefully made up, eyes a greenish-blue. Then, as now, my hair was as pale as sand, as smooth as a seashell, the unfussy style reflecting the roundness of my face. My mouth is a full rosebud, my nose classical; my complexion has always been admired. Naturally, there were laughter lines that summer, but my skin, though no longer the skin of a girl, had worn well and my voice had not yet acquired the husky depths that steal away femininity. In Italy men who were strangers to me still gave me a second look, although naturally not with the same excitement as once men did in other places where I've lived. I had, in truth, become more than a little plump, and though perhaps I should have dressed with such a consideration in mind this is something I have never been able to bring myself to do: I cannot resist just a hint of drama in my clothes – though not bright colours, which I abhor. 'I never knew a girl dress herself up so prettily,' a man who sat on the board of a carpet business used to say, and my tendency to put on a pound or two has not been without admirers. A bag of bones Mrs Chubbs was, according to her husband, which is why – so I've always suspected – he took to me in the first place.

Having read so far, you'll probably be surprised to learn that I'm a woman who prays. When I was a child I went to Sunday school and had a picture of Jesus on a donkey above my bed. In the Café Rose in Ombubu I interested Poor Boy Abraham in praying also, the only person I have ever influenced in this way. 'He's retarded, that boy,' Quinty used to say in his joky way, careless as to whether or not the boy was within earshot. Quinty's like that, as you'll discover.

I am the author of a series of fictional romances, composed in my middle age after my arrival in this house. I am no longer active in that field, and did not ever presume to intrude myself into the world of literature – though, in fairness to veracity, I must allow that my modest works dissect with some success the tangled emotions of which they treat. That they have given pleasure I am assured by those kind enough to write in appreciation. They have helped; they have whiled away the time. I can honestly state that I intended no more, and I believe you'll find I am an honest woman.

But to begin at the beginning. I was born on the upper stairway of a lodging-house in an English seaside resort. My father owned a Wall of Death; my mother, travelling the country with him, participated in the entertainment by standing upright on the pillion of his motor-cycle while he raced it round the rickety enclosure. I never knew either of them. According to the only account I have – that of Mrs Trice, who had it from the lodging-house keeper – my mother was on her way to the first-floor lavatory when she was taken with child, if you'll forgive that way of putting it. Within minutes an infant's cries were heard on the stairway. 'That was a setback,' Mrs Trice explained, and further revealed that in her opinion my father and mother had counted on my mother's continuing performance on the motor-cycle pillion to 'do the trick'. By this she meant I would be stillborn, since efforts at aborting had failed. It was because I wasn't that the arrangement was made with Mr and Mrs Trice, of 21 Prince Albert Street, in that same seaside town.

They were a childless couple who had long ago abandoned hope of parenthood: they paid for the infant that was not wanted, the bargain being that all rights were thereby relinquished and that no visit to 21 Prince Albert Street would ever be attempted by the natural parents. Although nobody understands more than I the necessity that caused those people of a Wall of Death to act as they did, to this day I fear abandonment, and have instinctively avoided it as a fictional subject. The girls of my romances were never left by lovers who took from them what they would. Mothers did not turn their backs on little children. Wives did not pitifully plead or in bitterness cuckold their husbands. The sombre side of things did not appeal to me; in my works I dealt in happiness ever after.

Quinty is familiar with my origins, for nothing can be kept from him. In Africa he knew I had accumulated money, probably how much. In 1978, when we had known one another for some time in Ombubu, it was he who suggested that I should buy a property in Umbria, which he would run for me as an informal hotel – quite different from the Café Rose. Repeatedly he pressed the notion upon me, tiring me with the steel of his gaze. Enough money had been made; there was no need for either of us to linger where we were. That was the statement in his eyes. We could both trade silence for silence in another kind of house. Half a child and half a rogue he is.

Quinty was born in the town of Skibbereen, in Ireland, approximately forty-two years ago. He is a lean man, with a light footstep, gaunt about the features. From the outer corner of each eye two long wrinkles run down his cheeks, like threads. When first I knew him in Ombubu he was shifty and unhealthy-looking. 'There's a sick man here,' Poor Boy Abraham cried, excited because a stranger had arrived at the café. I never knew where it was that Quinty had come from in Africa, or what had brought him to the continent in the first place. But I later heard, the way one does in an outpost like Ombubu, that several years before he'd tricked into marriage the daughter of a well-to-do Italian family, whom he had come across when she was an au pair girl in London. She ran away from him when she discovered that he was *not* the manager of a meat-extract factory, as he had claimed, and that he stole his clothes from D. H. Evans. He followed her to Modena, bothering her and threatening, until one night her father and two of her brothers drove him a little way towards Parma, pushed him out on to a grass verge and left him there.

He did not attempt to return, but that was how he came to be in Italy and learned the language. When first he mentioned Umbria to me I'd no idea where it was; I doubt I'd even heard of it. 'Let me have just a little money,' he begged in Ombubu one damply oppressive afternoon. 'Enough for the journey and then to look about.' Africa had gone stale for me, he said, which was a delicate way of putting it; the regulars at the Café Rose had not changed for years. In other words, the place had become a bore for both of us.

He sang the praises of Italy; I listened to descriptions of Umbrian landscape and hill-towns, of seasons bringing their variation of food and wine. Quinty can be persuasive, and I was happy enough to agree that a time of my life had come to an end. He'd played a certain role during most of that time, I have to say in fairness, and I have to give him credit for it. When he raised the subject of Italy I did the simplest thing: I gave him the money, believing I'd never see him again. But he returned a fortnight later and spread out photographs of Umbria and of villas that might be purchased. 'No one would care to die in the Café Rose,' he pointed out, a sentiment with which I could not but concur. One house in particular he was keen on.

Imagine a yellowish building at the end of a track that is in places like a riverbed. White with dust unless rain has darkened it, this track is two hundred metres long, curving through a landscape of olive trees and cypresses. In summer, broom and laburnum daub the clover slopes, poppies and geraniums sprinkle the meadows. Behind the house the hill continues to rise gently, and there's a field of sunflowers. The great lake of Trasimeno is on our doorstep; only thirty kilometres to the south there's a railway junction at Chiusi, which is convenient; and in the same area there's a health spa at Chianciano. In Quinty's photographs of the house there were out-buildings, and machinery that had rusted, but all that has changed since.

Of the house itself, the window shutters are a faded green, and the entrance doors – always open in the daytime – are green also. Further doors – glass decoratively framed with metal – separate the outside hall from the inner, and the floors of both, and of the dining-room and drawing-room – called by Quinty the *salotto* – are tiled, a shade of pale terracotta. Upstairs, on either side of two long, cool corridors, the bedrooms are small and simple, like convent cells. All are cream-distempered, with inside shutters instead of curtains, each with a dressing-table, a wardrobe and a bed, and a reproduction of a different Annunciation above each wash-stand. What luxury there is in my house belongs to the antique furniture of the downstairs rooms and the inner hall: embroidered sofas, pale chairs and tables, inlaid writing-desks, footstools, glass-fronted bookcases, the dining-room's chandelier.

When the tourists come to my house they pull the bell-chain and the sound echoes from the outer hall. Then Quinty, in his trim white jacket, answers the summons. 'Well?' he says in English, for one of his quirks is not immediately to speak Italian to strangers. 'How can I help you?' And the tourists cobble together what English they can, if it happens not to be their native tongue.

A handful of travellers is all Quinty ever makes welcome at a time, people who have spilled over from the hotels of the town that lies five kilometres away. A small, middle-aged woman called Signora Bardini, dressed always and entirely in black, is employed to cook. And Quinty found Rosa Crevelli, a long-legged, dark-skinned maid, to assist him in the dining-room. He presents us to our visitors as a private household, not at all in a commercial line of business. From the outset my house was known neither as an *albergo* nor a *pensione*, nor a restaurant with rooms, nor an hotel. 'This is what suits?' he suggested.

Being profitable, it was what suited Quinty, but for other

reasons it suited me also. Once, somewhere, I have seen a painted frieze continuing around the inside walls of a church – people processing in old-fashioned dress, proceeding on their way to Heaven or to Hell, I'm not sure which. Over the years the tourists who have come to my house have lingered in my memory like that. I see their faces, and even sometimes still hear their voices: tall Dutch people, the stylish French, Germans who brought with them jars of breakfast food, Americans delighting in simple things as much as children do, English couples suffering from digestive troubles. Chapters of books have been read, postcards written, bridge played in the evenings, even pictures painted, on the terrace. I have suffered no bad debts, nor have there ever been complaints about the bedrooms or the food. Quinty gave Rosa Crevelli English lessons and took up something else with her in private, but I asked no questions. Instead, within a month of settling in this house, I taught myself to type.

All this began nine years before the summer of which I write – the nine years in which I left the past behind, as title succeeded title: *Precious September*, *Flight to Enchantment*, *For Ever More*, *Behold My Heart!* and many others. My savings had bought the house; now – though after difficult beginnings – there was wealth. One day it would be Quinty who woke up rich, yet he could not possibly have predicted what would happen here: that I would sit down in my private room and compose romances. As far as Quinty knew, there was nothing in my history to suggest such a development; I was not that kind of woman. To tell the truth, I'd hardly have guessed it myself. As a villa hostess in an idyllic setting, I would make a living for both of us out of a passing tourist trade, as I had made one in a different role in Africa. That's how Quinty saw the future and as far as it went he was right, of course. He's cute as a fox when it comes to matters of gain, that being his life really.

Besides the tourists, our visitors are rare: a functionary from the tax office, or would-be thieves arriving with some excuse to look the place over, a traveller in fertilizers seeking directions to a nearby farm. Ever since the summer of 1987, which I think of to this day as the summer of the General and Otmar and the child, and which I remember most vividly of all the seasons of my life, nothing has been quite the same. That summer and for a few summers after it no tourists were received. Yet had you, for some other reason, gained admission during that summer Quinty would have led you through the outer hall and through the inner one and into the *salotto*, to wait there for me. Depending upon the time of day, the General would probably have been reading his English newspaper in the cool of the shadows, the child engrossed in one of her drawings, Otmar soundlessly tapping a surface with his remaining fingers. Many times that summer I imagined a voice saying: 'I have come for Otmar,' or: 'I understand you are keeping an old Englishman here,' or: 'Gather up the child's belongings.' Many times I imagined the car that had drawn up, and the dust its wheels had raised. I imagined a little knot of official people outside our entrance doors, one of them lighting a cigarette to pass the time, the butt later thrown down on the gravel. In fact, it wasn't like that in the least. All that happened was that Thomas Riversmith came.

That summer the child was eight years old, Otmar twenty-seven, the General elderly. They were three people on their own, and so was I. 'Heart's companion' is an expression I used to some effect in *Two on a Sunbeam*, and the fact that it lingers still in my mind, so long after the last paragraph of that work was completed, is perhaps significant, personally. I have always been the first to admit that in this world we are eternal beggars – yet it is also true that alms are not withheld for ever. When I was in the care of Mr and Mrs Trice I longed for a cowboy to step down from the screen of the old Gaiety

Cinema and snatch me on to his saddle, spiriting me away from 21 Prince Albert Street. When I was a girl, serving clerks in a public-house dining-room, I longed for a young man of good family to draw his car up beside me on the street. When I was a woman I longed for a different kind of stranger to appear in the Café Rose. That summer, in Umbria, I had long ago abandoned hope. In my fifty-sixth year I had come to terms with stuff like that. My stories were a help, no point in denying it.

The winter and the spring that preceded that summer had been quiet. From time to time bundles of fan mail had arrived, forwarded by the English publishers. There had been invitations to attend get-togethers of one kind or another – I remember in particular a title that struck me, a 'Festival of Romance', in some Iron Curtain country. I have never gone in for that kind of thing, and politely declined. A man wrote from New Zealand, pointing out that he enjoyed the same surname as one of my characters – an unusual name, he suggested, which indeed it was: I imagined I had invented it. A schoolgirl in Stockton-on-Tees poured out her heart, as schoolgirls often do. An elderly person chided me for some historical carelessness or other, too slight to signify.

In January a pet died. Years ago a lame Siamese cat had wandered into the grounds one day, a pathetic creature, all skin and bone. Signora Bardini befriended her. She called the creature Tata and attached a little bell on a chain around her neck so that a gentle tinkling became a feature of my house. We watched her health recovering, her coat becoming silky again, contentment returning. But Tata was never young and never sprightly: we knew from the beginning that all she could give us was what remained of a mostly spent life. She grew old gracefully, which is nice, I think, for any creature, human or otherwise. Signora Bardini put a little wooden board up, that being her way.

Signora Bardini is a widow to whom no children were born. When her husband, a carpenter by trade, died in 1975 she apparently took some time to come to terms with her solitude. Although she speaks no English, I believe she was not happy again until she came to work in my house. Her life might have been perfect here were it not for Quinty, towards whom from the first she displayed an undemonstrative antipathy. Clearly she does not care for his relationship with Rosa Crevelli, nor his cheese-paring in household matters. But Signora Bardini is not, and never was, a woman to raise any kind of fuss.

That, then, was how things were at the beginning of the summer I write of. The house smelt faintly of paint, for some redecoration had recently been completed. 'We must have a garden,' I had repeatedly said that winter and spring, saying it mainly to myself. 'It is ridiculous that a house like this does not have a garden to it.' That was a little on my mind, as it had been for years. One April, passing through a railway station here in Italy, I noticed a great display of azaleas in pots. I did not then know what that flower is called, but later described it to Quinty, who found out for me. Ever since I had longed for an azalea garden, and for the lawns that I remember in England, and for little flowerbeds edged with pinks.

You may consider I was fortunate to lack only a garden and a particular friend, and of course you are right. I was, and am, immensely fortunate. Not many of us acquire the means necessary to occupy a place such as this, to choose as I may choose, rarely to count the cost. Not many pass a winter and spring with only the death of a lame cat to grieve over. In the eyes of the tourists who came here I was a comfortably-off Englishwoman, well looked after by my servants. Quinty no doubt struck them as eccentric, if not bizarre. For one thing he has a way of arbitrarily allocating to other people a particular obsession in order to hold forth on it himself. From encyclopaedias and newspapers he has acquired a wealth of chatty information on many subjects – royal families, the Iron Age, sewerage systems, land speed records, the initiation practices of blind Amazon tribes. A score of times I have heard him supplying some unfortunate tourist with the history of the Japanese railways or the nature of the jackal. 'Giuseppe Garibaldi gave his name to a biscuit,' he has confided in my hall; 'the city of Bath to another. Hard tack the first biscuit of all was called, and had to be broken with a hammer.' Jauntily gregarious, he endlessly leant against a pillar in the *salotto* that summer to conduct with the General a one-sided conversation about sport. When Mr Riversmith arrived he was imbued with an interest in holy women, although it could hardly have been clearer that Mr Riversmith's subject was ants.

In other ways Quinty can be dubious to a degree that makes him untrustworthy. One day in the April of that year Rosa Crevelli was rude to me in Italian, scornfully curling down her beautiful lower lip as she muttered something. Quinty observed this, but did not reprimand her. For the first time, I realized, he must have broken the unspoken agreement that had existed between us ever since we'd left the Café Rose: he had told this girl about the past.

Later I taxed him with this treachery. He laughed at first, but then he turned away and his cheeks were damp with tears when again he faced me. 'How can you make such an accusation?' he whispered in a broken voice, and went on for so long – professing loyalty and faithfulness, uttering statements to the effect that he and the girl would lay down their lives for me, and protesting their desire to be nowhere else on earth but in my house – that I forgave him. 'I've poured you a nice g and t,' he said with a smile, coming to find me that evening in the *salotto*. When I met her next Rosa Crevelli curtsied.

Of course I could not be certain: maybe they sniggered, who can say? That I have a tendency to give the benefit of the doubt is either a weakness or a strength, but whichever it is I certainly don't claim it as a virtue. In fact, for very good reasons, I claim very little for myself: there's not much to me, and I'm the first to confess it. Nor do I claim anything mystical for that particular summer, no angels making their presence felt in my house, no voices heard. The child was an ordinary child, and I believe the others were ordinary too. Yet I don't think anyone would deny that it was a singular summer, and constituted an experience not given to everyone.

On 5 May, in the morning, wearing a suit of narrow black-and-white stripes, handbag and shoes to match, I left my house to travel to Milan. Quinty drove me to the railway junction and gave me my ticket on the platform. I can manage to travel very well on my own, despite my limited understanding of the Italian language. I recognize the familiar phrase when the ticket collector demands to see my ticket. In Rinascente and all the other stores I shop successfully, and in the Grand Hotel Duomo, where I always stay, excellent English is spoken. I look forward to shopping for clothes and shoes, taking my time over their choosing, going away to think things over, returning twice or three times: all that I love.

No one was staying in my house that day; no tourists had been sent on by the hotels since the end of last year's season, and we didn't expect any until the middle of June at least. Not that it is ever necessary for me to be there when visitors do arrive, but even so I like to welcome them. In the dining-room we sit at one round table and if English is spoken we talk of this and that, of places that have been visited, of experiences while travelling. If English is difficult for my guests, they speak in whatever language their own is, and I am not offended. There are never more than five in my dining-room or at the table on the terrace when we choose to dine outside.

In the train I imagined Quinty driving from the railway

junction and shopping in the town, the large, grey, open-hooded car parked in the shade of the chestnut trees by the church. He would call in for a coffee and then return to the house, where he and Signora Bardini and Rosa Crevelli would have lunch in the kitchen. I imagined them there, the three of them around the table, Quinty repeating new English words and phrases for Rosa Crevelli. I wondered if Signora Bardini, too, had also been told about the past. Determinedly I pushed all that away, and then my mind became occupied by a title that had occurred to me at the railway junction. *Ceaseless Tears*. So far, that was all I had. A heroine had not come to me: I could not even faintly glimpse a hero. Yet that title insisted itself upon my consciousness, and I knew that when a title was insistent I must persevere.

The train was a Rome express; it had come through Orvieto before I boarded it; Arezzo and Florence lay ahead. Imagine the stylish interior of a First Class *rapido*, the pleasant Pullman atmosphere, the frilled white antimacassars, the comfortable roominess. Diagonally across from where I sat were a young man and a girl: you could tell from their faces that they were lovers. An older couple travelled with the father of the woman: you could tell that was the relationship from their conversation. This threesome spoke in English, the lovers in German. A mother and a father travelled with their two children, a boy and a girl: I could not hear what they said, but everything about them suggested Americans. A woman who might have been in the fashion world was on her own. Italian businessmen in lightweight suits occupied the other seats.

I watched the lovers. He stroked her bare arm; you could tell how much she was in love with him, though he wasn't exactly handsome or even prepossessing. Did the older couple find the father a tiresome addition to their relationship? If they did, their politeness allowed not a single intimation of it to show; but, oddly, that politeness worried me. The Americans were stylish, the children arguing a little as spirited children do, the parents softly conversing, sometimes laughing. The mother was a particularly appealing young woman, fair-haired and freckled, with dimples in both cheeks and a flash of humour in her eyes.

Increasingly, I liked the title that had come to me, yet could still find no meaning in it, no indication of this direction or that. I recalled Ernestine French-Wyn, who had caused Adam to weep so in *Behold My Heart!* But one story rarely prompts the secrets of another and to avoid the nagging of my frustration I forced myself to observe again my fellow-travellers. The heads of the lovers were now bent over a scrap of paper on which the girl – she had a look of Lilli Palmer in her earliest films – was making a calculation. The daughter and son-in-law read; the old man had taken his watch off and was meticulously re-setting it. The little American boy was being reprimanded by his mother; the little girl changed places with him and took her father's hand. Somewhere in my mind's vision a description of this scene appeared: darkly-typed lines on the green typing paper I always use. I had no idea why that was.

The train moved swiftly, flashing through small railway stations and landscape still verdant after the rains of spring. The ticket collector appeared. Then the restaurant-car conductor hurried by, tinkling his midday bell. The businessmen went to lunch, so did the fashion woman. Out of nowhere, words came: *In the garden the geraniums were in flower. Through scented twilight the girl in the white dress walked with a step as light as a morning cobweb. That evening she hadn't a care in the world.*

It would go on. I would sit down at my little black Olympia and paragraph would obediently follow paragraph, one scene flowing into the next, conversations occurring naturally. I turned the pages of *Oggi*, but soon lost interest. Where would

I be, I found myself thinking, if late in my life I had not discovered my modest gift? At my age there were women who still served clerks their plates of food in public-house dining-rooms. There were women who sold shoes – as I have also done – or swabbed out cabins on ferry-steamers. It had never seemed like good fortune that I'd found myself in the Café Rose, but in fairness to fate I have to say it was. I ran the place in the end – everyone's friend, as they used to say there. I was fortunate, I must record again, because without the Café Rose I don't believe I'd ever have put pen to paper.

I must have slept, for in a dream Ernie Chubbs approached me outside the Al Fresco Club and exclaimed, just as he had in reality, 'Hi, sugar!' He told me he loved me in the Al Fresco Club; he wanted to sit with me all night, he whispered. Ernie went on buying drinks, the way they liked you to in the Al Fresco, and when another man came up and bought drinks also Ernie was furious, and told him to go away. Then, as abruptly as it always is in dreams, I was shopping in Milan, trying on long suede coats in different colours – next season's cut, the assistant said. I liked the wrap-around style and was saying so when my eyes were wrenched open by a burst of noise. There was glass in the air, and the face of the American woman was upside down. There was screaming, and pain, before the darkness came.

2

'It's Quinty come to see you,' Quinty said. 'You're all right. You're OK.'

He tried to smile. The lines on his cheeks had wrinkled into zigzags, but the smile itself would not properly come.

'Is it Good Friday?' I asked, confused, because Good Friday did not come into any of it. I heard myself talking about the Café Rose, how one particular Good Friday the Austrian ivory cutter had been high on the stuff he took, and Poor Boy Abraham had been upset on account of anyone being high on the day when Jesus suffered on the Cross.

There were hours of shadows then – they might have been years for all I knew – and through them moved the white uniforms of the nurses, one nurse in particular, with thinning black hair. 'You've had a bang,' Quinty said, 'but thanks be to God you're progressing well.' He sniffed the way he sometimes does, a casual, careless sound, disguising something else.

'What happened?' I asked, but Quinty's reply – if he made one at all – eluded me, and when I looked he was no longer there. I didn't want to think; I allowed my mind to wander where it would, gliding over the past, swooping into it here and there, no effort made on my part, no exhaustion. 'Have they paid?' Mrs Trice asked her husband. She was always asking him that, he being a collector of insurance money. 'You're weak with them,' she accused him. 'Weak as old water.' As a child, I lived for eight years at 21 Prince Albert

Street before I realized that my presence there was the result of a monetary transaction. I'd always addressed the Trices as though they were my mother and father, not knowing about the people of the Wall of Death until Mrs Trice told me in the kitchen one Saturday morning. 'They were paid a sum by Mr Trice,' was how she put it. 'They weren't people you'd care for.'

Between sleep and consciousness the honest black face of Poor Boy Abraham edged out the Trices, his negroid features intent as he swept the veranda floor at the Café Rose, while the fans whirred and rattled. The four Englishmen played poker at the corner table. 'Where would I be if I did not come with my woes to you?' the Austrian ivory cutter asked and, as always, drew the conversation round to his hopeless coveting of some black man's wife. The aviator who was a regular in the café had been a skywriter, advertising a brand of beer mainly.

I dropped into sleep and dreamed, as I had on the train. 'Feeling better, girlie?' Ernie Chubbs was solicitous in Idaho. 'Fancy a chow mein sent up?'

A nurse spoke kindly in Italian. I could tell she was being kind from her expression. She rearranged my pillows and for a moment held my hand. I think I must have called out in my sleep. When I seemed calm again she went away.

When Ernie Chubbs suggested accompanying him to Idaho I did so because I wanted to see the Old West. To this day, the Old West fascinates me: Claire Trevor in her cowgirl clothes, Marlene Dietrich singing in the saloon. To this day, I close my eyes when a wheel of the stagecoach works itself loose; I'm still not quick enough to see a sheriff draw his gun. Mr Trice took me to the Gaiety Cinema on Sunday afternoons and we would watch the comedy short – Leon Errol or Laurel and Hardy, or Charlie Chase – and then the Gaumont News and the serial episode, and whatever else there was besides the main feature. Sometimes the main feature was a gangster thriller, or an ice-skating drama or a musical, and that was always a disappointment. I longed for the canyons and the ranches, for the sound of a posse's hooves, the saddles that became pillows beneath the stars.

Idaho was a disappointment too. Ernie Chubbs, who said he knew the region well, assured me it was where the Old West still was; but needless to say that wasn't true. A lifetime's dream was shattered – not that I expected to find the winding trails just as they had been shown to me, but at least there might have been something reminiscent of them, at least there might have been a smell of leather. 'You're simple, Emily,' the big doctor who came to the Café Rose used to say. And yes, I suppose I am: I cannot help myself. I'm simple and I'm sentimental.

'How long is it?' I asked. 'How long have I lain here?'

But the Italian nurses only smiled and rearranged my pillows. I worried about how long it was; yet a moment later – or perhaps it wasn't a moment – that didn't matter in the least. The Idaho of Ernie Chubbs – his going out on business, the waiting in the motel room – must have made me moan, because the nurses comforted me again. When they did, the Old West filled my thoughts, driving everything else away. In the Gaiety Cinema there were no curtains to the screen. On to the bare, pale expanse came the holsters and the sweat-bands of the huge-brimmed hats, the feathered Indians falling one by one, the rough and tumble of the fist fights. I was seven, and eight, and nine, when Dietrich sang. '*See what the boys in the back room will have,*' she commanded in her peremptory manner, '*And tell them I'll have the same.*' In my sedated tranquillity I heard that song again; and the Idaho of Ernie Chubbs seemed gone for ever. Young men I have myself given life to whispered lines of love to happy girls. The Wedding March played, bouquets were thrown by brides. The Café Rose might not have existed either.

*

'Quinty.'

'Rest yourself, now.'

'There were other people. A young man and his girl who talked in German. Americans. Italians in dark suits. A woman in the fashion business. Three English people. Are they here too, Quinty?'

'They are of course.'

'Quinty, will you find out? Find out and tell me. Please.'

'Don't upset yourself with that type of thing.'

'Are they dead, Quinty?'

'I'll ask.'

But he didn't move away from my bedside. He visited me to see if there were grounds for hope, promise of a relapse. His eyes were like two black gimlets; I closed my own. Little Bonny Maye was employed in Toupe's Better Value Store, attaching prices to the shelved goods with a price-gun. Small discs of adhesive paper, each marked with an appropriate figure, were punched on to the surface of cans and packets. At certain hours of the day she worked a till.

Little Bonny Maye was taken up by Dorothy, an older girl from the table-tennis club. Dorothy was secretary to a financier and had been privately educated. Her voice was beautiful, and so was Dorothy herself. Bonny couldn't think why she'd been taken up, and even if Dorothy had a way of asking her to do things for her rather a lot Bonny still appreciated the friendship more than any she had known. She was only too grateful: all the time with Dorothy that was what Bonny thought. Her single anxiety was that some silliness on her part would ruin everything.

'Did you ever read that story of mine, Quinty? *Little Bonny Maye*?' I was surprised to hear myself asking Quinty that. It wasn't our usual kind of conversation. He said:

'It's great you have your stories.'

'I thought about them in the Café Rose.'

'You told me that.'

'I don't remember telling you.'

'You had a drink or two in, the time you told me.'

The three words of the title were blue on the amber of the book-jacket, the two girls illustrated below. I must have said so because Quinty nodded. Soon afterwards he went away. He might even have guessed I had begun to hear the girls' voices.

'Dear, there is an "h" in "house", you know.' Dorothy could bring out Bonny's blushes, hardly making an effort. When they went on holiday together, while Bonny fetched and carried for the older girl, Dorothy drew up a list of words that Bonny should take special care with. 'Our fork belongs on our plate, not in the air. I had a nanny who said that.'

When I dozed, the pain in my face sometimes dulled to a tightness and for the first time, probably, I tried to smile. The two girls were on holiday in Menton, and when Blane came into their lives he naturally took Dorothy out, leaving poor Bonny to mooch about on her own, since it wouldn't have been right for her to tag along. 'Of course I don't mind. Of course not.' She tried to keep her spirits up by eating ice-cream or going to look at the yachts.

I was aware of making no effort whatsoever. I controlled nothing. Faces and words and voices flowed over me. 'Such an unhappy thing!' Blane exclaimed. 'Such rotten luck!' Dorothy had developed appendicitis. An ambulance had come. 'You need a cognac,' Blane insisted. 'Or a Cointreau. No, Bonny, I absolutely insist. Poor girl, how wretched for you too!' Dorothy's holiday was a write-off. Every morning Blane called for Bonny in his Peugeot and drove her to the bedside of her friend, who usually had made a list of things she wanted. Afterwards Blane and Bonny lunched together in the Petit Escargot.

Three months ago Blane had inherited Mara Hall, a great house in its own park in Shropshire. But as soon as he had done so he left England, being fearful of the house even though he loved it.

'My mother died when I was one and a half. There was always just my father and myself.'

'No brothers or sisters, Blane?'

'No brothers or sisters.'

Bonny thought how lonely that must have been: a boy growing up in a great house with only his father and the servants for company. His father was severe, expecting a lot of his heir.

'I'm a coward, I dare say. I'd give the world to take everything in my stride. I'm running away. I know that, Bonny.'

'Was your father – '

'My father did things perfectly. He was a strong man. He married the woman he loved and never looked at another. The servants and his tenants adored him.'

There was a head gardener at Mara Hall, and several under-gardeners. There was a butler and a cook and old retainers in the way of maids, all of whom had been there as long as Blane could remember. Once there'd been footmen, but that was ages ago.

Mara Hall was more vivid than the shadows of nurses whose speech I did not understand, and the odour of anaesthetic: the lawns and the tea roses, the mellow brick of the house itself and of the kitchen-garden walls, the old ornamental ironwork. I felt as Bonny felt – overawed with wonder. Bonny had not been abandoned in a bleak seaside town by a couple who rode a Wall of Death; but something like it was in Bonny's past, even if it did not come out in the story. I felt that strongly now; I never had before.

'It sounds so lovely, Blane. Your home.'

'Yes, it's lovely.'

They walked in the evenings on the promenade. He would marry Dorothy, Bonny thought, and take her to Mara Hall.

Dorothy was capable as well as beautiful. Dorothy would gently lead him back to his responsibilities. He would become as strong as his father; he would do things as perfectly.

'Dear Bonny,' he said, in a tone that made her hold her breath. She could not speak. The sea was a sheet of glass, reflecting the tranquil azure of the sky. 'Dear Bonny,' he said again.

The doctors who attended me conferred. One spoke in English, smiling, telling me I had made progress, saying they were pleased.

'I'm glad you're pleased,' I replied.

'You have been courageous, signora,' the same doctor said. 'And patient, signora.'

They passed on, both nodding a satisfied farewell at me. Blane took the modest creature's arm; she trembled at the touch because no man had ever taken Bonny Maye's arm before. No man had ever called her dear. She'd never known a heart's companion.

'Much better,' Dorothy said, but it was their last day in Menton. She'd left her dark glasses on her bedside table and Bonny went to fetch them. Blane drove her to Bordighera and Bonny miserably ate an ice-cream on the front. She wrote the postcards she should have written before, to the other girls in Toupe's Better Value Store. She'd be back before they received them.

Once only the story was interrupted by the ravenous features of Ernie Chubbs, his eyes seeking mine from the shadows of the Al Fresco Club, his fingers undoing my zips in the motel room. There was an old mangle in the motel room, and a tin bath in which kindling was kept. I knew all that was wrong. 'It wouldn't do to tell,' Ernie Chubbs said. 'Good girls don't tell, Emily.' That was wrong also. It wasn't Ernie who'd ever said good girls don't tell, and Ernie Chubbs hadn't been ravenous in that particular way.

The chill fag-end of a nightmare, darkly colourless, something like a rat in a drawing-room, went as quickly as it had arrived, crushed out of existence by a warmer potency. 'Well, really!' Dorothy was a little cross when they returned from Bordighera. She lay down to rest and complained that the bedroom was too hot and then, when the window was opened, that the draught was uncomfortable. She wanted Vichy water but they brought her Evian. Impatiently she stubbed out a cigarette she had not yet placed between her lips.

'Bonny,' he said, leaning on the open door of the little Peugeot. 'Oh, Bonny, if I could only make you happy!'

He is the kindest person I have ever known, she thought. He knows I love him; he knows I have been unable to help myself. This is kindness now, to speak of my happiness when it is his and Dorothy's that is at stake. They have had a little tiff this afternoon, but soon they will make it up. Tonight he will ask Dorothy to marry him, and after tomorrow I shall never in my life see either of them again. Dorothy'll be too busy and too full of happiness ever to return to the table-tennis club. There'll be the wedding preparations and then the honeymoon and then the return to Mara Hall.

'Look, Bonny,' he said, and in the sunlight sapphires sparkled. He had snapped open a little box; the slender band of gold that held the jewels lay on a tiny cushion. 'I bought it for her,' he said, 'three days after we met.'

'It's beautiful.' The words choked out of her. Tears misted her vision. She tried to smile but could not.

'I have to tell you that, Bonny. I have to tell you I bought it for Dorothy.'

She nodded bleakly.

'I might have offered it to Dorothy this afternoon. I could not, Bonny.'

Again she nodded, not understanding, trying to pretend she did.

'I can only love you, Bonny. I know that, if I know nothing else in this world.'

'Me? *Me?*'

'Yes. Oh yes, my dear.'

His face was smiling down at her bewilderment. His lips were parted. She heard herself saying she was nothing much, while knowing she should not say that. She heard him laugh.

'Oh, but of course you are, my dear. You are everything in this world to me. Darling, you are the sun and the stars, you are the scent of summer jasmine. Can you understand that?'

She flushed and looked away, thinking of Dorothy and feeling treacherous, and more confused than ever. She wanted to laugh and cry all at once.

'Darling Bonny, you have the lips of an angel.'

His own touched the lips he spoke of. The gentle pressure was like fire between them.

'Oh Blane, Blane,' she murmured.

'Say nothing, darling,' he whispered back, and in some secret moment the sapphire ring found her engagement finger.

I would like to have married and had children. But Ernie Chubbs, swearing to me that he took precautions, never did so. In my association with him I had no fewer than four abortions, the last of them in Idaho. I would not have children now, they told me then. 'Sorry, girlie,' Ernie Chubbs said. 'Fancy a chilli con carne sent up?'

Crimson spread on denim. A hand that was crimson also bounced back from the ceiling, dangled for an instant in the air, fingers splayed. A screeching of terror was different from the screams of pain. Even while it was happening you could hear the difference.

'Twenty pound,' Mrs Trice said. 'That's what he give. He likes a child, Mr Trice does. He got the dog for nothing.' Rough type of people she said, to profit from a baby. 'You bloody give it back,' I said to him, 'but they was gone by then. Fifty they ask, twenty he give.' Rum and Coca-Cola, Ernie asked for in the Al Fresco, a fiver a time. 'Easy money,' Mrs Trice said, lifting a slice of Dundee to her lips. 'Travelling people's always after easy money.'

'Lightning,' I said myself. 'The train was struck by lightning.'

The strength of the drugs was daily reduced; tranquillity receded little by little. At 21 Prince Albert Street I stirred milk in a saucepan, and Mrs Trice was furious because the milk burnt and milk cannot burn, apparently, while it is stirred. It was in the back-yard shed at 21 Prince Albert Street that the mangle was, and the kindling in the bath. It was in the back-yard shed that the man I took to be my father wept and said we mustn't tell, that good girls didn't. It was his face that was ravenous, not Ernie Chubbs's. Ernie loved me was what I thought.

Mr Trice possessed a smooth-haired fox terrier, a black and white dog of inordinate stupidity. With the chopping of kindling, washing up, and frying the breakfast, a task when I was nine was to exercise this animal, which refused to leave the confined space of the Trices' back-yard of its own accord. It would amble reluctantly behind me down Prince Albert Street and on the damp sand of the seashore. Seagulls would sniff it when I sat with my back against a breakwater and it stood obediently on the sand. They sometimes even poked at it with their beaks, but the dog displayed signs neither of alarm nor pleasure, seeming almost to be unaware of the seagulls' attention. When other dogs ran snarling up to it Mr Trice's pet stolidly sat there, unimpressed also by this display of hostility. If actually attacked, it would cringe unemotionally, tightly pressed to the ground, eyes closed, hackles undisturbed. 'A gentle creature,' Mr Trice would say if he had chosen to accompany me, which now and again, to my dismay, he did.

We would walk by the edge of the sea and Mr Trice would attempt to entice his pet towards the grey waves. But it always stubbornly resisted the temptation of the stones that were thrown and the whistles of encouragement that emanated from Mr Trice. 'It's a sign of intelligence,' he would remark in defeat. 'There's many a dog doesn't spot cold water before he's in it.' Mr Trice and I sat down by the breakwater and he always glanced over his shoulder before he put his arm around me to cuddle me. 'Tell your Daddy you love him,' he would urge, and I did as I was bidden, thinking it would be unobliging not to. Mr Trice would glance about him again. He would hold my hand and kiss the side of my forehead while the dog stood beside us, not seeming to know it would be restful to sit down also. The cuddles and the kisses were all Mr Trice ever went in for on the seashore. In the back-yard shed he took me on to his knee, and in the darkness of the Gaiety Cinema he kept a hand on my leg for all the time we were there, all the way through *Destry Rides Again* and *Stagecoach War*. It wasn't until later, when I was eleven, that Mr Trice took me into the bedroom when Mrs Trice was out at the laundry where she worked. He gave me a penny and I promised. People got the wrong end of the stick, he said.

Lying in that Italian hospital, I had no wish to dwell upon the uglier parts of my life yet could not prevent myself from doing so. In my fifty-sixth year, I had my beautiful house, and as I lay there that was where I endeavoured to see myself. But again my thoughts betrayed me. Wholly against my will, I was snagged in another kind of ugliness, keeping company with the tourists who over the years had gathered at my table. The mother and the nervous son, the homosexuals with Aids, the *ménage à trois* and all the others: so many tell-tale signs there were, in gesture or intonation. Long ago the mother had instilled fear in her son in order to keep him by her. The younger of the homosexuals had been unfaithful but was forgiven; both soon would die. The women who shared a lover had each settled for second best. In my dining-room or on the terrace Rosa Crevelli filled the tourists' wineglasses and offered them fruit or *dolce*. Wearily I rose from my table, drained by such human tragedy.

How joyfully then, how warmly, I kept company with pert Polly Darling or Annette St Claire! From pretty lips, or lips a little moist, poured whispers and murmurs and cries of simple delight. Dark hair framed another oval face, eyes were as blue as early-summer cornflowers. Often it was half-past three or four before I replaced the cover of my black Olympia. New light streaked the sky when I smoked, on the terrace, the last of the night's cigarettes. A lovely tiredness cried out for sleep.

They dabbed at my forehead. They bound the blood-pressure thing around my arm. They stuck in a thermometer. Their tweezers pulled out stitches.

'No harm in secrets,' Mr Trice said. 'No harm, eh?'

'No.'

After the third time he'd given me a penny I put the chair against my bedroom door, but it didn't do any good. So on the day before my sixteenth birthday I packed a brown cardboard suitcase, and left five shillings in its place because the suitcase was Mrs Trice's and we'd been taught not to take things at Sunday school.

'Let's have a look at you,' the woman in the public house said. 'Have you served at table before?'

I never had, so they put me in the kitchen first, washing up the dishes. 'Gawky,' the woman said. 'God, you're a gawky girl.' My hair was frizzy, I couldn't keep my weight down, my clothes were bought in second-hand places mostly. Yet not much time went by before other men besides Mr Trice desired me and gave me presents.

*

'A timed device,' Quinty said.

'I thought it was lightning.'

'It was a timed device.'

'Where was it, Quinty? Near where I was?'

'It was close all right. The rest of the train was OK.'

'Is that why the police came?'

'That would be it.'

Early on in my hospital sojourn the *carabinieri* had been clustered round my bed. Their presence had interfered with my dreams and the confusion of my thoughts. Their dark blue uniforms trimmed with red and white, revolvers in black holsters, the grizzled head of one of them: all this remained with me after they had left my bedside, slipping in and out of my crowded fantasies. If conversation took place I do not recall it.

Later, in ordinary suits, detectives came with an interpreter. There were several visits, but soon it became clear from the detectives' demeanour they did not consider it likely that I, in particular, had been the target of the outrage, though they listened intently to their interpreter's rendering of my replies. A hundred times, it seems like now, they asked me if I had noticed anything unusual, either as I stepped on to the train or after I occupied my seat. Repeatedly I shook my head. I could recall no one skulking, no sudden turning away of a head, no hiding of a face. Each time, the detectives were patient and polite.

'*Buongiorno, signora. Grazie.*'

'Good day, lady,' the interpreter each time translated. 'Thank you.'

Carrozza 219 our carriage had been. I remembered the number on the ticket. Seat 11. In my mind's vision the faces of the people who'd been near me lingered: the American family, the lovers, the couple and their elderly relative. The fashion lady and the businessmen in lightweight suits had gone to lunch.

'They are here,' Quinty said, and glanced at me, and added: 'Some of them.'

Of the three English people, only the old man was alive. Of the German couple, only the boy. In the hospital they called the little American girl Aimée: the family passport had been found. She was the sole survivor of that family, and there was difficulty in locating someone in America to take responsibility. It even seemed, so Quinty said at first, that such a person did not exist. The information that filtered through the *carabinieri* and the hospital staff appeared to indicate that there were grandparents somewhere, later that there was an aunt. Then we learnt that the child's grandfather suffered a heart condition and could not be told of the loss of his son, his daughter-in-law and a grandchild; the grandmother could not be told because she would not be able to hide her grief from him. Lying there, I approved of that: it was right that these people should be left in peace; it was only humane that elderly people should be permitted to drift out of life without this final nightmare to torment them.

'They're having difficulty in tracking down the aunt they're after,' Quinty reported. 'It seems she's travelling herself.'

She was in Germany or England, it was said, but the next day Quinty contradicted that. It was someone else who was travelling, a friend of the family who'd been assumed to be this relation. The aunt had been located.

'Unfortunately she can't look after a child.'

'Why not, Quinty?'

'It isn't said why not. Maybe she's delicate. Maybe she has work that keeps her on the go all over the place.'

I thought about this after he'd gone. I wondered what kind of a woman this could be, who, for whatever reason, could be so harsh.

'They got it all wrong again,' Quinty said on a later

occasion. 'That woman's the aunt of someone else. The same story with those grandparents.'

I wouldn't have known any of this if Quinty hadn't been interested in questioning the *carabinieri* on the matter. From what I could gather, the policemen did not themselves appear to know what was happening in the search – so far away – for possible relatives or family friends. The hospital authorities were worried because the child would not, or could not, speak.

Apart from the victims of Carrozza 219 no one on the train had been injured, and no one of political importance had been on the train in any case. The old man's son-in-law had had something to do with a merchant bank apparently; the American father had been a paediatrician. Yet a bomb had been planted, deliberately to take life, ingeniously and callously placed where those who by chance had been allocated certain seats would be killed or maimed.

What would one see, I wondered, in the perpetrators' eyes? What monstrous nature did such human beings seek to disguise? There'd been crime, often more than petty, on the S.S. *Hamburg*. Living human embryos had been scraped out of my body and dropped into waste-disposal buckets. Seedy confessions had surfaced in the Café Rose. An ugly guilt had skittered about in the shifty eyes of Ernie Chubbs. Yet no crime could rank with what had happened on the train I'd caught at 11.45 on the morning of 5 May 1987. In search of consolation, I wrote down the few lines I had composed in Carrozza 219, the beginning of the work which had come to me through its title. *In the garden the geraniums were in flower. Through scented twilight the girl in the white dress walked with a step as light as a morning cobweb. That evening she hadn't a care in the world.* But I found it difficult to continue and did my best, instead, simply to recover.

The old man and I suffered from shock. I'd had splinters of glass taken from the left side of my face; he from his legs and body. The German boy, called Otmar, had lost an arm. The old man was a general.

'An irony,' he murmured in the corridor where he learned to walk again. 'It was I who'd reached the end of things.'

He made the statement without emotion. I remembered his daughter as a pretty woman in a gentle, English kind of way, quiet and rather slight, a little faded. Aries probably.

'We are fortunate to be alive, General.'

He turned away his head, half shaking it as he did so. I told him about the child called Aimée, about the search for relatives in America. I hoped to involve him in the pathos of the child's predicament and perhaps to make him realize that someone else had lost even more than he had. He did his best to respond, later even to smile. With military stoicism he appeared to be resigned to what had occurred, his vocation no doubt demanding that. A sense of melancholy did not come from him, only one of weariness. I left him soldiering on, precisely obeying the nurses' strictures, marching with the aid of a metal stick, back and forth between his bed and a curtained balcony at the corridor's end.

'I'm sorry, Otmar,' I commiserated, and in a soft whisper, speaking quite good English, the German boy accepted the sympathy: that it was offered because of the loss of his sweetheart or a limb was barely relevant. In the train he had been wearing a red and yellow lumberjack shirt and rather large glasses, which were shattered in the blast. He wore other spectacles now, wire-rimmed, and jeans and a plain grey shirt. His features were sallow, the eyes behind the magnifying lenses still terrified. Unlike the General, he did not attempt to smile. There was a cornered look about Otmar, as if the horror he had woken up to was too much for him.

'We must hope, Otmar. What there is left to us is hope.'

Every time I returned to my own room, and to the ward when I was a little better, I endeavoured to proceed with my new work, but still I found it difficult to continue. This had never happened before: with reason, I had been confident on the train as soon as the girl appeared in my mind's vision. Yet now it seemed as though a film had halted within seconds of its commencement. The fluttering of the girl's dress was frozen, her carefree mood arrested in a random instant. Was there some companion of whom my broken cinematograph held the secret, some figure waiting to step from the garden's shadows? Would the carefree mood become ecstatic? Would a gardenia nestle in the long fair hair? I did not know. I knew neither what joy nor sorrow there was; my girl was nameless, without detail in her life, vague as to parentage, born beneath a choice of all the stars. The title *Ceaseless Tears* appeared so naturally to belong to the suffering on the train that greater bewilderment, and blankness, was engendered. I was aware of a sensation that caused me to shiver in dismay, as though all that had been given to me had been snatched away. Then one day Quinty said:

'They could stay a while in the house, you know.'

A week ago the General had murmured that he would find the return to England difficult, and wished he did not have to face it immediately. 'The struggle back and forth,' he said. 'The bed, the corridor, the holy statue in the wall, the balcony. The faces of the patients, the smell of ether. You feel that's where you belong.'

Quinty was clearly out to profit from misfortune, but even so I saw nothing to object to in his suggestion. 'You would find it peaceful,' I told the old man. 'My house is high enough to be cool. Sometimes a breeze blows over the water of Lake Trasimeno.'

He nodded, and then he thanked me. When he sought me out two days later I explained that we were used to catering for strangers, that for many years we had taken in passing tourists when the hotels of the neighbourhood were full.

'I would insist on paying,' he gently laid down. 'I told the man I would insist on paying whatever rates you normally charge.'

'It is he who sees to all that.'

I'd known army officers of lower rank before; never a general. He had the look of one, sparely made, his hair the colour of iron, great firmness about the mouth, a grey moustache. He was a man of presence, but of course he was not young: touching seventy, I guessed.

'A week or two,' he agreed with unemphatic graciousness. 'That would be nice. But are you certain, Mrs Delahunty? I don't want to be a nuisance at a time like this.'

'Indeed I'm certain.'

Otmar refused at first. Poor boy, with every day that passed he seemed more wretchedly unhappy and I sensed that, even more than the General, he did not know how to return to the world he was familiar with.

'You are most good.' His voice echoed the distortion in his eyes. Often, in speaking to him, I found myself obliged to turn my head away. 'But it should not be. I have not money to pay this.'

Quinty cannot have known that, and I resolved, if necessary, to pay for Otmar's stay myself. I said the money didn't matter. Some time in the future, when everything had calmed for him, he could pay a little. 'If you would care to, Otmar, the house is there.'

The doctor who looked after the American child was a Dr Innocenti, a small, brown-complexioned man with gold in his teeth. He was the English-speaking one among the doctors and the nurses, and had often acted as interpreter for the specialists who were more directly concerned with the General and Otmar and myself. When he heard that hospitality had been offered in my house he came to see me and to thank me.

'It will do some good,' he said. 'I would prescribe it.'

He wore a pale brown suit and a silk tie, striped red and green. When I said the child also would be welcome in my house he doubtfully shook his head. The *carabinieri* would have to be consulted, he explained, since the child – being at present without a guardian – was in their charge. 'In Italy we must always be patient,' he said. 'But truly I would wish the little girl removed from the hospital ambience.'

'Is she recovering, doctor?'

In reply the little shoulders were raised within the well-cut suit. The hands gesticulated, the nut-brown head sloped this way and then that.

'Slowly?' I prompted.

Too slowly, a contortion of the neat features indicated: it was not easy. At present the prognosis was not good.

'The child is more than welcome if you believe it would be a help.'

'So Signor Quinty explain to me. There is nowhere else, you comprehend.' He spoke gently. His jet-black eyes were as soft as a kitten's. Piscean, I guessed. 'I will speak with the officers of the *carabinieri*. Red tape may be cut, after all. To be surrounded by people whose language she understands will be advantageous for Aimée.'

Later I learnt he'd been successful in persuading the *carabinieri* to agree to his wishes. They would visit us two or three times a week to satisfy themselves that the child remained safely in our care, and report their satisfaction to the American authorities. Dr Innocenti himself would also visit us regularly; if there were signs of deterioration in the child she would be at once returned to the hospital. But he believed that the clinical surroundings were keeping the tragedy fresh in her mind and preventing her from coming to terms with it.

'You are generous, signora. I have explained to Signor Quinty the expenses will be paid when the person they seek in

America is found. My friends of the *carabinieri* have reason to believe that this is not a poor family.'

We were all discharged on the same afternoon and the first night in my house we sat around the tiled table on the terrace, the General on my right, Otmar on my other side. The child was already sleeping in her bed.

Rosa Crevelli brought us lasagne, and lamb with rosemary, and the Vino Nobile of Montepulciano, and peaches. A stranger would have been surprised to see us, with our bandages and plaster, the walking wounded at table. I was the only one who had not lost a loved one, having none to lose. As I dwelt upon that, the title that had come to me floated through my consciousness, golden letters on a stark black ground. I saw again a girl in white passing through a garden, and again the image froze.

3

Miss Alzapiedi, our Sunday-school teacher, was excessively tall and lanky, with hair that was a nuisance to her, and other disadvantages too. It was she who gave me the picture of Jesus on a donkey to hang above my bed; it was she who taught me how to pray, pointing out that some people are drawn to prayer, some are not. 'Pray for love,' Miss Alzapiedi adjured. 'Pray for protection.'

So before I ran away from 21 Prince Albert Street I prayed for protection because I knew I'd need it. I prayed for protection when I worked in the public-house dining-room and the shoe shop and on the S.S. *Hamburg*, and when Ernie Chubbs took me to Idaho, and later when he abandoned me in Ombubu. Even though I was trying to be a sophisticate it didn't embarrass me to get down on my knees the way Miss Alzapiedi had taught us, even if there was a visitor in the room. To be honest, I don't get down on my knees any more. I pray standing up now, or sitting, and I don't whisper either; I do it in my mind.

At the end of my first year in this house I finished *Precious September*. I wrote it just for fun, to pass the time. When it was complete I put it in a drawer and began another story, which this time I called *Flight to Enchantment*. Then glancing one day through the belongings of a tourist who was staying here, I came across a romance that seemed no better than my own. I noted the publisher's address and later wrapped

Precious September up and posted it to England. So many months passed without a response that I imagined the parcel had gone astray or that the publisher was no longer in business. Then, when I had given up all hope of ever seeing my manuscript again, it was returned. *We have no use for material of this nature*, a printed note brusquely declared. I knew of no other publisher, so I continued with *Flight to Enchantment* and after a month or so dispatched it in the same direction. This elicited a note to the effect that the work would only be returned to me if I forwarded a money order to cover the postage. When that wound had healed I completed another story quite quickly and although it, too, was similarly rejected I did not lose heart. There was, after all, consolation to be found in the tapestries I so very privately stitched. They came out of nothing, literally out of emptiness. Even then I marvelled over that.

We are interested in your novelette. I found it hard to believe that I was reading this simple typewritten statement, that I was not asleep and dreaming. The letter, which was brief, was signed *J. A. Makers*, and I at once responded, impatient to receive what this Makers called 'our reader's suggestions for introducing a little more thrust into the plot'. These arrived within a fortnight, a long page of ideas, all of which I most willingly incorporated. Eventually I received from J. A. Makers an effusively complimentary letter. By now many others among his employees had read the work; all, without exception, were overwhelmed. *We foretell a profitable relationship*, Mr Makers concluded, foretelling correctly. But when I received, after I'd submitted the next title, a list of 'our reader's suggestions' I tore it up and have never been bothered in that way since. That story was *Behold My Heart!* Its predecessors, so disdainfully rejected once, were published in rapid succession.

Something of all this, in order to keep a conversation going,

I passed on to the General. I knew that conversation was what he needed; otherwise I would have been happy to leave him in peace. I wanted to create a little introduction, as it were, so that I might ask him to tell me about his own life.

'If you would like to,' I gently added.

He did not at once reply. His gnarled grey head had fallen low between his shoulders. The *Daily Telegraph* which Quinty had bought for him was open on his knees. My eye caught gruesome headlines. A baby had been taken from its pram outside a shop and buried in nearby woods. A dentist had taken advantage of his women patients. A bishop was in some other trouble.

'It sometimes helps to talk a bit.'

'Eh?'

'Only if you'd like to.'

Again there was a silence. I imagined him in his heyday, leading his men in battle. I calculated that the Second World War would have been his time. I saw him in the desert, a young fox who was now an old one.

'You're on your own, General?'

'Since my wife died.'

His eyes passed over the unpleasant headlines in the newspaper. There was something about a handful of jam thrown at the prime minister.

'Things were to change when we returned,' he said.

I smiled encouragingly. I did not say a word.

'I was to live with my daughter and her husband in Hampshire.'

He was away then, and I could feel it doing him good. Only one child had been born to him, the daughter he spoke of, that faded prettiness on the train. 'Don't go spoiling her,' his wife had pleaded, and he told me of a day when his daughter, at six or seven, had fallen out of a tree. He'd lifted her himself into the dining-room and covered her with a rug on the sofa.

She'd been no weight at all. 'This is Digby,' she introduced years later while they stood, all four of them drinking gin and French, beneath that very same tree.

'I couldn't like him,' he confessed, his voice gruff beneath the shame induced by death. I remembered the trio's politeness on the train, the feeling of constraint, of something hidden. I waited patiently while he rummaged among his thoughts and when he spoke again the gruffness was still there. If the outrage hadn't occurred he would have continued to keep his own counsel concerning the man his daughter had married: you could tell that easily.

He spoke fondly of his wife. When she died there'd been a feeling of relief because the pain was over for her. Her departure from him was part of his existence now, a fact like an appendix scar. When I looked away, and banished from my mind the spare old body that carried in it somewhere an elusive chip of shrapnel, I saw, in sunshine on a shorn lawn, a medal pinned on a young man's tunic and a girl's arms around a soldier's neck. 'Oh, yes! Oh, yes!' she eagerly agreed when marriage was proposed, her tears of happiness staining the leather of a shoulder strap. You could search for ever for a nicer man, she privately reflected: I guessed that easily also.

'No, I never liked him and my wife was cross with me for that. She was a better mother than I ever was a father.'

Again the silence. Had he perished in the outrage he would have rated an obituary of reasonable length in the English newspapers. His wife, no doubt, had passed on without a trace of such attention; his daughter and his son-in-law too.

'I doubted if I could live with him. But I kept that to myself.'

'A trial run, your holiday? Was that it?'

'Perhaps so.'

I smiled and did not press him. Jealousy, he supposed it was. More than ever on this holiday he had noticed it – in *pensiones* and churches and art galleries, permeating every conversation. No children had been born to his daughter, he revealed; his wife had regretted that, he hadn't himself.

'Have you finished with the *Telegraph*, sir?' Quinty hovered, not wishing to pick up the newspaper from the old man's knees. Rosa Crevelli set out the contents of a tea-tray.

'Yes, I've finished with it.'

'Then I'll take it to the kitchen, sir, if I may. There's nothing I like better than an hour with the *Telegraph* in the cool of the evening. When the dinner's all been and done with, the *Telegraph* goes down a treat.'

A glass of lemon tea, on a saucer, was placed on a table within the General's reach. Rosa Crevelli picked up her tray. Quinty still hovered. Nothing could stop him now.

'I mention it, sir, so that if you require the paper you would know where it is.'

The General acknowledged this. Quinty softly coughed. He inquired:

'Do you follow the cricket at all, sir?'

The General shook his head. But noticing that Quinty waited expectantly for a verbal response, he courteously added that cricket had never greatly interested him.

'Myself, I follow all sport, sir. There is no sport I do not take an interest in. Ice-hockey. Baseball. Lacrosse, both men's and women's. I have watched the racing of canoes.'

The General sipped his tea. There were little biscuits, *ricciarelli*, on a plate. Quinty offered them. He mentioned the game of *boules*, and again the racing of canoes. I made a sign at him, endeavouring to communicate that his playfulness, though harmless, was out of place in an atmosphere of mourning. He took no notice of my gesture.

'To tell you the truth, sir, I'm an armchair observer myself. I never played a ball-game. Cards was as far as I got.'

Quinty's smile is a twisted little thing, and he was smiling now. Was he aware that the reference to cards would trigger a memory – the Englishmen, and he himself, playing poker at the corner table of the Café Rose? Impossible to tell.

'I'm afraid he's a law unto himself,' I explained as lightly as I could when he had left the room. A tourist had once asked me if Quinty had a screw loose, and for all I knew the General was wondering the same thing, too polite to put it into words. By way of further explanation I might have touched upon Quinty's unfortunate life, how he had passed himself off as the manager of a meat-extract factory in order to impress an au pair girl. I might have told how he'd been left on the roadside a few kilometres outside the town of Modena, how later he'd turned up in Ombubu. I might even have confessed that I'd once felt so sorry for Quinty I'd taken him into my arms and stroked his head.

'It's just his way,' I said instead, and in a moment Quinty returned and asked me if he should pour me a g and t, keeping his voice low, as if some naughtiness were afoot. He didn't wait for my response but poured the drink as he stood there. Half a child and half a rogue, as I have said before.

Deep within what seemed like plumage, a mass of creatures darted. Their heads were the heads of human beings, their hands and feet misshapen. There was frenzy in their movement, as though they struggled against the landscape they belonged to, that forest of pale quills and silky foliage.

For a week I watched with trepidation while the child created this world that was her own. Signora Bardini had bought her crayons when we noticed she'd begun to draw, and then, with colour, everything came startlingly alive. Mouths retched. Eyes stared distractedly. Cats, as thin as razors, scavenged among human entrails; the flesh was plucked from dogs and horses. Birds lay in their own blood; rabbits were devoured by maggots.

Sometimes the child looked up from her task, and even slightly smiled, as though the unease belonged to her pictures, not to her. Her silence continued.

In her lifetime Otmar's mother had made lace. He told me about that, his remaining fingers forever caressing whatever surface there was. His mother had found it a restful occupation, her concentration lost in the intricacies of a pattern. He spoke a lot about his mother. He described a dimly lit house in a German suburb, where the furniture loomed heavily and there was waxen fruit on a sideboard dish. Listening to his awkward voice, I heard as well the clock ticking in the curtained dining-room, the clock itself flanked by two bronze horsemen. Schweinsbrust was served, and good wine of the Rhine. '*Guten Appetit!*' Otmar's father exclaimed. How I, at Otmar's age, would have loved the house and the family he spoke of, apfelstrudel by a winter fireside!

'Madeleine,' Otmar said, speaking now of the girl who had died in the outrage. I told him she had reminded me of a famous actress, Lilli Palmer, perhaps before his time. I recollected, as I spoke, the scratchy copy of *Beware of Pity* that had arrived in Ombubu in the 1960s, the film seeming dated and old-fashioned by then.

'Madeleine, too, was Jewish,' Otmar said, and I realized I'd been wrong to assume the film actress was not known to him.

They'd been on their way from Orvieto to Milan. Otmar was to continue by train to Germany, Madeleine to fly from Linata Airport to Israel, where her parents were. For weeks they'd talked about that, about whether or not she should seek her father's permission to marry. If he gave it he might also give them money to help them on their way, even though Otmar was not Jewish himself, which would be a disappointment. 'When the day comes you wish to marry you must seek his permission,' her mother had warned Madeleine years ago. 'Otherwise he will be harsh.' Her father had left Germany for Jerusalem five years ago, offering his wealth and his business acumen to the land he regarded as his spiritual home. Madeleine had never been there, but when she wrote to say she wished to visit her family her father sent a banker's draft, its generosity reflecting his pleasure. 'So we afford the expensive train,' Otmar explained. 'Otherwise it would be to hitchhike.'

I did not say anything. I did not say that surely it would have been more sensible to travel to Rome to catch a plane, since Rome is closer to Orvieto than Milan is. I was reminded of the General revealing to me that he and his daughter and son-in-law had originally intended to travel the day before, and of the businessmen and the fashion woman going to the dining-car. Otmar went on talking, about the girl and the days before the outrage, the waiting for the banker's draft and its arrival. In August they would have married.

'The kraut hasn't any money,' Quinty said in his joky way. 'He's having us on.'

'He told me he hadn't any money. I'll pay what's owing.'

'You're not running a charity, don't forget.'

'I'm sorry for these people.'

I might have reminded Quinty that once I'd been sorry for him too. I might have reminded him that I had been sorry for Rosa Crevelli when first she came to my house, ill-nourished and thin as fuse-wire, her fingernails all broken. I'd been sorry for the cat that came wandering in.

'You'll get your reward in heaven,' Quinty said.

That summer I opened my eyes at a quarter past five every morning and wished there were birds to listen to, but the summer was too far advanced. Dawn is bleak without the chittering of birds; and perhaps because of it I began, at that particular time, to wonder again about the perpetrators. No political group had claimed responsibility, and the police were considering a theory that we had possibly been the victims of a lunatic. Naturally I endeavoured to imagine this wretched individual, protected now by a mother who had always believed that one day he would commit an unthinkable crime, or even by a wife who could not turn her back on him. What kind of lunatic, or devil? I wondered. What form of mental sickness, or malignancy, orders the death of strangers on a train? In the early morning I took my pick of murderers – the crazed, the cruel, the embittered, the tormented, the despised, the vengeful. Was it already a joke somewhere that six were dead and four maimed, that a child had been left an orphan, her own self taken from her too? The cuts on my face and body would heal and scarcely leave a scar: I'd been assured of that, and did not doubt it. But in other ways neither I nor any of the others had recovered and I wondered if we ever would. The ceaseless tears of my title mocked me now; still understanding nothing, I felt defeated.

We were in a nowhere land in my house: there was a sense of waiting without knowing in the least what we were waiting for. Grief, pain, distress, long silences, the still shadows of death, our private nightmares: all that was what we shared without words, without sharing's consolation. Ghosts you might have called us had you visited my house in Umbria that summer.

The police came regularly. Two *carabinieri* remained outside by the police car while the detectives asked their questions and showed us photographs of suspects. Signora Bardini carried out iced tea to the uniformed men. Every day Dr Innocenti spent some time with the child, his presence so quiet in the house that often we didn't notice he was there. Time, he always said – we must have faith in time.

In my private room I opened the glass-faced cabinet where my titles are arranged, and displayed for Aimée the pleasantly colourful jackets in the hope that they'd influence the hours she spent with her crayons. Obediently she examined the illustrations and even nodded over them. She opened one or two of the books themselves, and appeared briefly to read what was written. But still she did not speak, and when she returned to her room it was to complete a picture full of horrors even more arresting than the previous ones. 'The appetite is good,' Dr Innocenti soothingly pointed out, and appeared to take some heart from that.

One night there was at least a development. A telephone call came from the American official who had several times visited the hospital in connection with the child's orphaning. He informed Quinty that a brother of Aimée's mother had been located in America. This time there was no mistake. Dr Innocenti had already spoken to the man.

'Isn't that good news?' I remarked to the General the following morning while we were breakfasting on the terrace.

'News? I beg your pardon?'

'They've found Aimée's uncle.'

'Oh.'

'Riversmith the name is.'

'There was a Riversmith at school.'

'This one's an American.'

The General was fond of the child; I had watched him becoming so. But he had difficulty in concentrating on the discovery of an uncle, and with hindsight I can see he didn't even want to think about this man. The conversation drifted about, edging away from the subject I had raised. He spoke of the Cotswold village near the boarding-school he'd mentioned, the warm brown stones, the little flower gardens. He and his friends could walk to the outskirts of the village, where a woman – a Mrs Patch – would give them tea in her small dining-room, charging sixpence for a table which seated four. Mrs Patch made lettuce sandwiches, and honey sandwiches, and sardine sandwiches; and there were hot currant scones on which the butter melted, and banana cake with chocolate filling, and as much tea as you wanted. It was a tradition, the walk to the village, the small dining-room of the cottage, the sixpenny piece placed on the tablecloth, and Mrs Patch saying she had sons of her own, now grown up. If you paid more – a shilling for a table for four – and if you gave her warning well in advance, Mrs Patch would cook fish.

These memories of time past were delivered in a tone that did not vary much. Jobson played the organ in the chapel. He played the voluntary while everyone stood in long pews, parallel to the aisle, waiting for the masters to process to their places behind the choir. Handel or Bach would thunder to a climax and then there'd be a fidgeting silence before the headmaster led the way. Sometimes, afterwards, Jobson revealed the errors he had made, but no one had noticed because Jobson was skilful at disguising his errors even as he made them. Jobson and the General had been friends from the moment they met, their first night in the Junior Dormitory.

Odd, I reflected as I listened, how an old man's memory operates in distress! Odd, the flotsam that has been caught and surfaces to assist him: the mustiness of Mrs Patch's dining-room, a prefect's voice, a mug dipped into a communal pail of milk. Housemasters – six older men – sprawled in splendour in the Chapel, a chin held in a hand, an arm thrown back, black gowns draping their crossed legs. While he spoke, the old man's gaze remained fixed on the distant hills. Remembered bells had different sounds: the Chapel bell, the School bell, the night-time bell. A conjuror came once and performed with rabbits and with birds. Boys smoked behind a gymnasium. Rules were broken, but no one stole. Owning up was taken for granted, and if you were caught you did not lie. At that school, modestly set in undemanding landscape, he said he'd learned what honour was. Again there was his effort at a smile, more successful now than in the hospital.

'Crewe and McMichael are being a nuisance,' he confided a little later, and for a moment I imagined the two he spoke of were boys, like Jobson, at the school. In all four of us bewilderment easily became confusion.

In fact, he referred to solicitors. Crewe and McMichael were his: Johnston Johnson his son-in-law's. Both firms had written to him. Having offered their commiserations, they turned now to wills and property, to affairs being tidied up, legalities of one kind or another. Soothingly, I said:

'They see it as their duty, I suppose.'

He nodded, half resigned to that, half questioning such duty. He spoke of the empty house in Hampshire and of his daughter's effects: he was the inheritor of both. He did not say so but I knew he dreaded going from room to room, opening drawers and cabinets. Pieces of jewellery had been named, to be given to the children of friends. A letter from one of the solicitors stated in a pernickety way that there might well be doubt as to which article was which. There were the son-in-law's belongings also, his collection of Chinese postage stamps, his photographs. There were the clothes of both of them, and books and records. *Articles of a personal nature,* the same solicitor had written. *We shall in the fullness of time need to take instruction regarding all these matters.*

'A friend of your daughter would sort the stuff out, you know.'

He said he didn't want to shirk what was expected of him. And yet I knew – for it was there in his face – that his soldier's courage faltered, probably for the first time in his life. He could not bear to see those clothes again, nor the house in Hampshire where he might now be living with his daughter and the man he hadn't cared for. How petty that small aversion seemed to him in retrospect! How petty not to have come to terms with a foible! His gaze slipped from the far-off hills; tired eyes, expressionless, were directed toward mine. Had his heart been full of that dislike as he fiddled with his watch in Carrozza 219? Had it nagged at him even while death occurred?

'Oh, my God,' he whispered, without emotion.

Tears were repressed, lost somewhere in that sudden exclamation. His grasp on consolation weakened, the Memory Lane of boyhood was useless dust. I reached for his hand, took it in both of mine, and held it. In that moment I would have given him whatever he asked of me.

'No one can help disliking a person.' I whispered also. 'Don't dwell on it.'

'All these years she must have guessed. All these years I hurt her.'

'Your daughter looked far too sensible to be hurt when it wasn't meant.'

'I couldn't stand his laugh.'

I imagined his wife standing up for their son-in-law, saying he wasn't bad, saying what was important was their daughter's happiness. How could it possibly matter that a laugh was irritating? 'Now, you behave yourself': her reprimand was firm, though never coming crossly from her. She managed people well.

'No, it wasn't meant,' he said. He slipped his hand away, but I knew he had experienced the comfort I intended. His voice had calmed. He was less huddled; even sitting down, his military bearing had returned.

'I wish they'd just dispose of everything,' he said with greater spirit.

'Well, perhaps they will.'

I smiled at him again. He needed an excuse, a cover for what he saw as cowardice. 'When in distress, pretend, my dear,' Lady Daysmith pronounces in *Precious September*, and I pretended now, suggesting that his reluctance to return to England was perhaps because England was so very different from the country it had been in his Cotswold days. Tourists I'd talked to complained of violence in the streets, and derelict cities, and greed. Jack-booted policemen scowled from motorcycles. In television advertisements there was a fashion for coarsely-spoken people, often appearing to be mentally afflicted. The back windows of motor-cars were decorated with snappy obscenities.

'I never noticed.' His interest was only momentarily held. He rarely watched the television, he confessed.

'Oh, I've been assured. Not once but many times. Cornerboys rule the roost in England's green and pleasant land. The Royals sell cheese for profit.'

Pursuing the diversion, I threw in that Ernie Chubbs had managed to get the royal warrant on the sanitary-ware he sold, that there'd been a bit of a fuss when it was discovered he was using it without authority. The General nodded, but I knew I'd lost him: in their grey offices the solicitors were already droning at him through pursed solicitors' lips. He stood forlorn among old books and box-files and sealed documents in out-trays. A lifetime's bravery oozed finally away to nothing.

'General, you're welcome to remain here for as long as you feel like it. You're not alone in this, you know.'

'That's a great kindness, Mrs Delahunty.' The beaten head was raised; again, blank eyes stared deeply into mine. 'Thank you so much,' the General said.

A conversation with Otmar was similar in a way. In the *salotto* I had just lit a cigarette when he entered and in his self-effacing way slipped into an armchair by the tall, wide-open french windows. I smiled at him. 'An uncle of Aimée's has been found,' I said. 'Isn't that good news at last?'

'Oh, *ja*.'

He nodded several times.

'*Ja,*' he said again.

I didn't press; I didn't try to draw enthusiasm from him. But the fact was that someone would love Aimée now; and in time Aimée herself would love. I didn't say to Otmar that there has to be love in a person's life, that no one can do without either receiving it or giving it. I didn't say that love, as much as a daughter and a girlfriend, had been taken away. I didn't say that love expired for me on a Wall of Death. 'They killed themselves in the end,' Mrs Trice callously replied when I asked. 'Stands to reason with a dangerous game like that.' A thousand times I have mourned the passing of the people who abandoned me, the motor-cycle skittering over the edge, smashing through the inadequate protection of a wooden rail. To this day, the woman's arm is still triumphantly raised in a salute. A red handkerchief still flies from her mouth, and the machine races on to nowhere.

'Where did you learn your English, Otmar?' I asked the question when I had poured the boy his coffee. I watched him awkwardly breaking a brioche.

'I learn in school. I was never in England or America.'

A finger ran back and forth on the edge of the saucer beneath his coffee cup. Once Madeleine had been in England, he said, working in some relation's business in Bournemouth. 'Silk scarves. At first she is in the factory, then later in the selling.'

For a moment it seemed he made an effort, as the General had, to contain his tears: his eyes evaded mine when he spoke of Madeleine. He dipped his brioche into his coffee and I watched him eating it. In answer to another question he said he'd had hopes of becoming a journalist. It was in this connection that he and Madeleine made the journey to Italy – because he'd heard so much about the murderer of lovers who was known in Florence as the Beast. The murders took place at night when couples made love in parked cars. Otmar had a theory about it and wanted to write an article in the hope that a Munich newspaper would print it. Following a lead, they travelled down to Orvieto and it was there they'd decided to get married, even though Otmar was penniless. It was in Orvieto that Madeleine had telephoned her father in Jerusalem.

'A cigarette?'

He took one and politely thanked me. It was the right arm that was gone. The coffee cup in his left hand, now placed on the table, was still unnatural. I smiled to make him feel a little more at ease. I lit my own cigarette and his, and as I did so my fingers brushed the back of his hand. I said:

'How did you meet her?'

'In a supermarket.'

She'd been reaching for a packet of herbs and had upset some jars of mustard. He had helped her to replace them, and later at the checkout they found themselves together again. 'Come and have a coffee,' he invited, and they walked through the car park and across a street to a café. I was reminded of the encounter in *Petals of a Summer*, but naturally I kept that to myself.

'These are good cigarettes,' Otmar remarked, rising as he spoke. 'I must walk now,' he said, and left me to my thoughts.

Such a romance had never occurred in Madeleine's life before. I imagined her saying that to herself as they strolled together to the café, he politely carrying the plastic bag that contained her supermarket groceries. In the café he confessed he'd seen her on previous occasions, that he had often seen her. He had bided his time, he confessed, and spoke with passion of her pretty features – how they had come into his dreams, how he had wondered about her voice. 'Oh, I'm not pretty in the very least,' she protested, but he took no notice. He said he was in love with her, using the word that had so endlessly been on the lips of the Austrian ivory cutter. *'Liebe,'*

Otmar repeated as they passed again through the car park. '*Liebe.*'

Madeleine could not sleep that night. She tossed and turned until the dawn. If there could be a pretence about her prettiness there could be none about his. He was not handsome, even a little ugly, she considered. Yet none of it mattered. Never before had she experienced such intense protestations, not just of love, but of adoration.

'*O Otmar, ich liebe dich,*' Madeleine said exactly a month later.

When Dr Innocenti came the next time he complimented Aimée on her latest drawings and then drew me aside. He spoke of her uncle, a professor of some kind apparently. Their conversation on the telephone had been a lengthy one.

'I have urged *il professore* that this tranquillity in your house should be maintained for a while longer. That she should not yet be returned to the United States.'

'Of course.'

'For the moment I oppose so long a journey for the child.' He paused. 'For you, signora, is inconvenient?'

'Aimée is more than welcome here.'

'You are generous, signora.'

'Doctor, what do you believe happened?'

'How, signora?'

'What was the reason for this crime? The police still come here.'

He shrugged in his expressive way, eyebrows and lips moving with his shoulders, his palms spread in a question mark.

'They still come because still they do not know.' The shrug went on. 'No one takes the blame.'

'There must be a reason for such an act. Somewhere there must be.'

'Signora, it is on all occasions the policy of our *carabinieri* to preserve a silence. They have the intention to entice forward some amateur tormented by their game.'

'Or a lunatic. I've heard that mentioned.'

'A clever lunatic, signora. A package that belongs to no one among the passengers placed on to a luggage rack. Terrorists, not lunatics, I think we guess.'

'But which one of us were they seeking to kill? These are just ordinary people.'

'Signora, which one did they seek to kill at Bologna? Angela Fresu, aged three?'

4

For the first time since the outrage I walked again in the early morning, on the roads that now and again turn into dusty-white tracks, among the olive shrubs and the broom. The line of the hills in the distance was softened by a haze that drained the sky of colour. Tiny clouds, like skilful touches in a painting, stayed motionless above the umbrella pines and cypresses that claim this landscape for Umbria.

I wondered about the American professor. As a name, Riversmith had a ring to it, but it told me nothing else. Its bearer was the brother of the dimpled, fair-haired woman on the train, which suggested a man in his thirties. When I thought about him, his face became like hers.

'*Buongiorno, signora!*' an old woman with a stack of wood on her back greeted me. Further on, her husband was cutting the grass of the verge with a hook. You don't meet many on the white roads; sometimes a young man rides by on an autocycle; in autumn the harvesters come for the grapes, in November for the olives. It was pleasant to walk there again.

'*Buongiorno, signora!*' I called back. Once I made a terrible mistake in Sunday school when giving an answer to a question, saying that Joseph was God. Someone began to titter and I could feel myself going red with embarrassment, but Miss Alzapiedi said no, that was an error anyone could make. Miss Alzapiedi's long chest was as flat as a table-top. Summer or winter, she never wore stockings, her white, bony ankles exposed to all weathers. It seemed a natural confusion to say that Joseph was God, Joseph being Jesus's father and God being the Father also. 'Of course.' Miss Alzapiedi nodded, and the tittering ceased.

I dare say remembering Sunday school was much the same as the General having tea in Mrs Patch's cottage and Otmar recalling the comfort of his parents' house. It was a way of coming to terms, of finding something to cling to in the muddle; I dare say it's natural that people would. In all my time at Miss Alzapiedi's Sunday school there was only that one uneasy moment, before Miss Alzapiedi stepped in with kindness. Otmar similarly recalled being reprimanded because he'd overturned a tin of paint when the decorators came to paint the staircase wall and the hall, and again when he stole a pear from the sideboard dish. There was a moment of embarrassment in the dormitory the old man had spoken of, with its rows of blue-blanketed beds and little boys in pyjamas. But these instances, dreadful at the time, were pleasant memories now.

'And they spread out palms before the donkey's feet,' Miss Alzapiedi said, and while she spoke you could easily see the figure of Jesus in his robes, with his long hair and his beard. The donkey was a sacred animal. 'You have only to note the cross on every donkey's back,' Miss Alzapiedi said. 'All your lives please note the black cross on that holy creature.'

The General had led his men to the battle-fronts of the world but always he'd returned to the girl he'd proposed to on a sunlit lawn, whose tears of joy had stained the leather of his uniform. He had not looked at other women. Amid the banter and camaraderie of the barracks his desires had never wandered, not even once, not even in the heat of the desert with the promise of desert women only a day or two away. His happy marriage was written in the geography of the old man's face, a simple statement: that for nearly a lifetime two people had been as one.

'Isn't that much better?' Otmar's mother said the first time he wore spectacles, when a world of blurred objects and drifting colours acquired precision. In the oculist's room he couldn't read the letters on the charts. The oculist had spectacles, too, and little red marks on the fat of his face, the left-hand side, close to the nose. When Otmar asked his mother if he'd always have to wear the spectacles now she nodded, and the oculist nodded also. When the oculist smiled his white teeth glistened. The mother's coat was made of fur.

It was Mary who began the business about donkeys, riding on one all the way to the stable of the inn. Joseph walked beside her, guiding the donkey's head, thinking about carpentry matters. Mary understood the conversation of angels. Joseph sawed wood and planed it smooth. He made doors and boxes and undertook repairs. To this day I can see Joseph's sandals and Jesus's bare feet, and the women washing them. To this day I can see Jesus on the holy donkey in the picture above my bed.

'Fragments make up a life, my dear,' Lady Daysmith says in *Precious September*. For the General, bodies lie where they have fallen on the sand, sunburnt flesh stiffening, soldiers from Rochester and Somerset. For the General, there are those gentle Cotswold bells, the organ booming, evening hymns. There is the beauty of virginity specially kept, to be given on a wedding night; and drinks beneath that tree the child fell out of. 'Darling,' the well-loved wife returns his love. 'Darling, you are so sweet to me.'

For me, there is the stolid dog, the dampness of the beach, the seagulls coming nearer. There are the searchlights of Twentieth-Century Fox, the soft roar of the lion, Western Electric Sound. In a room a man removes an artificial leg and pauses to massage the stump. Across a street a neon sign flashes red, then green, all through a half-forgotten night. First thing of all, there's a broken floor-tile, brownish, smooth.

Why is there fear left over in Otmar's eyes, behind the

spectacles? Does some greater ordeal continue, some private awfulness? In the supermarket the girl's hand reaches again into the shelves. The adoration in the car park and the café is an ecstasy in its first bright moment. *Liebe! Liebe!* Eyes close, fingers touch. But something is missing in all this; there is some mystery.

Years after her time as a Sunday-school teacher Miss Alzapiedi becomes Lady Daysmith – shortened to a reasonable height, supplied with hair that isn't a nuisance, given a bosom. Lady Daysmith is old of course, Miss Alzapiedi was scarcely twenty in the Sunday school. But a plain girl can grow old gracefully, why ever not? 'The peepshow of memory is what I mean by fragments': I hadn't been in my house more than a month before I caused the woman who had been the Sunday-school girl to utter so.

In the soft warmth of that early morning I paused on the track that led to the heights behind my house. I looked back at the house itself, in that moment acutely aware of how the malignancy of the act had reached out into us, draining so much from the old man, rooting itself in Otmar, leaving sickness with the child. Then I pushed all that away from me and tried once more, though without success, to find a beginning for *Ceaseless Tears*. I strolled on a little way before finally turning back.

'I have always wanted a garden here,' I remarked to Otmar on the terrace less than an hour later. We smoked together. I asked him if there'd been a garden at his parents' house and he said yes, a small back garden, shady in summertime, a place to take a book to. You could tell from the way he spoke that his mother and father were no longer alive. I don't know why I wondered if this fact was somehow related to the fear that haunted him. I did so none the less.

*

'Where is this?' the child asked, suddenly, a week after my first walk on the white roads. She had been engrossed in one of her pictures, stretched out on the floor. The blinds were drawn a little down for coolness, but there was light enough in the *salotto*.

'Where is this?' Aimée asked again.

The General was sitting with his newspaper, near the windows. Otmar had just entered the room. Neither of them spoke. Eventually I said:

'You are in my house, Aimée. I am Mrs Delahunty.'

She did not directly reply, but said that her mother was cross because there'd been a quarrel in the yard. Girls couldn't be robbers, her brother Richard insisted, because he wanted to be the robber himself. As if speaking to herself, the child explained that she was to be the old woman who hadn't the strength to get up from her sun chair when the robber walked in and asked where the safe was. But she was always the old woman; all you did was lie there. She continued to draw the foreleg of a dog that did not seem to be alive. She shaded its hollow stomach. She and her brother had tried to guess, on the train-station platform, what two Italians were saying to one another. The woman of the pair was angry. The man had forgotten to lock the windows of their house, Aimée guessed.

'I should think that was so,' I said.

'That woman was mad at him.'

It was difficult to know if she spoke in response to what I'd said or not. A frown gathered on her freckled forehead. Her flaxen hair, so like her mother's, trailed smoothly down her back. Her eyes, lit for the while she spoke, went dead again.

'Your uncle's coming, Aimée. Mr Riversmith.'

But she was colouring now, lightly passing the crayons over the misshapen limbs and bodies. The tip of her tongue protruded slightly, in concentration.

'Mr Riversmith,' I said again.

Still there was no response. Otmar left the room, and I guessed he had gone to ask Quinty to summon Dr Innocenti.

'Your uncle,' the General said.

Aimée spoke again, about another game she and her brother had played, and then, with the same abruptness, she ceased. She said nothing more, but those few moments of communication had more than a slight effect on both the General and Otmar, and in a sense on me. This spark had kindled something in us; the brief transformation fluttered life into a hope that had not been there before. At last there was something good, happening in the present. At last we could reach out from our preoccupation with ourselves alone.

The General smiled at Aimée, while she sat there on the floor, lost to us again. Aimée was a lovely name, I said, not knowing what else to say. 'Thank God for this,' the General murmured, to me directly.

'Yes, thank God.'

Otmar returned to the room and sat with us in silence, and in time we heard Dr Innocenti's car approaching. We didn't break the silence, but listened to the hum of the engine as it came closer, until eventually the tyres scrunched on the gravel outside.

'*Coraggio!*' Dr Innocenti said, speaking softly from the doorway, not coming quite into the room. '*Va meglio, vero.*'

Later he predicted that Aimée would make progress now, but warned us that on the way to recovery there might be disturbances. It was as well to expect this since often the return to reality could be alarming for a child: you had only to consider what this reality was, he pointed out. His hope was that Aimée would not be too badly affected. He charged us with vigilance.

The days and weeks that followed were happy. Diffidently, I put it to Dr Innocenti that the child was the surviving fledgling in a rifled nest, her bright face the exorcist of our pain. The beauty that was promised her, and already gathering in those features, was surely to be set against the torn limbs in Carrozza 219, against the blood still dripping from the broken glass, the severed hand like an ornament in the air? Her chatter challenged the old man's guilt and was listened to, as wisdom might be, by Otmar. *'Si. Si,'* Dr Innocenti several times repeated, hearing me out and appearing to be moved.

Local people, learning that some victims of the outrage were in my house, sent gifts – flowers and wine, fruit, *panettone*. The *carabinieri* came less often now, once in a while to ensure that Aimée was still being looked after, then not at all, instead making their inquiries of Dr Innocenti. Once I walked into the kitchen to find Signora Bardini weeping, and thought at first she suffered some distress, but when she lifted her head I saw that her streaming eyes gleamed with joy. Naturally no such display of emotion could be expected of Quinty, though Rosa Crevelli was affected, of that I'm certain. 'Aimée! Aimée!' she called about the house.

Perhaps for the General Aimée became a daughter with whom he might begin again. Perhaps for Otmar she was the girl who had died on the train. I do not know; I am not qualified to say; I never asked them. But for my own part I can claim without reservation that I became as devoted to the child during that time as any mother could be. It was enough to see her sprawled on the floor with her crayons, or making a little edifice out of stones near where the car was kept, or drinking Signora Bardini's iced tea. Aimée shuffled in and out of a darkness, remaining with us for longer periods as these weeks went by. Sometimes she would sit close to me on the terrace, and in the cool of the evening I would stroke her fine, beautiful hair.

5

The telephone in my house rings quietly, but never goes unheard because there is a receiver in the hall and in the kitchen, as well as in my writing-room. It was I myself, in my private room, who answered it when eventually Aimée's uncle rang.

'Mrs Delahunty?'

'Yes.'

'Mrs Delahunty, this is Thomas Riversmith.'

'How d'you do, Mr Riversmith.'

'May I inquire how Aimée is?' He sounded as if grit had got into his vocal cords – a tight, unfriendly voice, unusual in an American.

'Aimée is beginning to return to us.'

'She speaks now every day?'

'Since the afternoon she spoke she has continued.'

'I've talked with your doctor many times.' There was a pause and then, with undisguised difficulty: 'I want to say, Mrs Delahunty, that I appreciate what you have done for my niece.'

'I have not done much.'

'May I ask you to tell me what the child says when she speaks to you?'

'In the first place she asked where she was. Several times she has mentioned her brother by name. And has spoken of being scolded by her mother.'

'Scolded?'

'As any child might be.'

'I see.'

'If Aimée wakes in the night, if there is a nightmare, anything like that, a cry of distress would be heard at once. Otmar sleeps with his door open. In the daytime there is always someone near at hand.'

At first there was no response. Then: 'Who is it that sleeps with a door open?'

'Otmar. A German victim of the outrage. Also in my house is an English general, similarly a victim.'

'I see.'

'It's strange for all of us.'

That observation was ignored. There was another pause, so long I thought we'd been cut off. But in time the gritty voice went on:

'The doctor seems anxious that the child should make more progress before I come to take her home.'

'Aimée is welcome to remain as long as is necessary.'

'I'm sorry. I did not catch that.'

I repeated what I'd said. Then formally, the tone still not giving an inch, socially or otherwise:

'Our authorities here have informed yours that I will naturally pay all that is owing. Not only the hospital fees, but also what is owing to yourself.'

This sounded like a speech, as though many people were being addressed. I did not explain that that was Quinty's department. I did not say anything at all. A woman's voice murmured in the background, and Mr Riversmith – having first questioned some remark made – asked if I, myself, was quite recovered from the ordeal. The background prompt was repeated; the man obediently commiserated. It had been a dreadful shock for him, he confessed. He'd read about these things, but had never believed that he himself could be brought so close to one. You could hear the effort in every word he spoke, as if he resented having to share a sentiment, as if anything as personal as a telephone conversation – even between strangers – was anathema to him.

'That is true, Mr Riversmith.'

The solemnity and the seriousness made me jittery. He was a man without a word of small talk. I knew he hadn't smiled during all this conversation. I could tell that smiling didn't interest him. Again I reflected that he wasn't at all like an American.

'If I may, I'll call again, Mrs Delahunty. And perhaps we might arrange a date that's convenient to both of us.'

He left a number in case of any emergency, not asking if I had a pencil handy. He had no children of his own: Dr Innocenti hadn't told me that, but I guessed it easily.

'Goodbye, Mr Riversmith.'

I imagined him replacing the receiver in its cradle and turning to the woman who had shadowed the encounter for him. In the lives of such men there is always such a woman, covering their small inadequacies.

'Not an easy person,' I remarked later to the General and Otmar – which I considered was a fair observation to make. I repeated as much of the conversation as I could recall, and described Thomas Riversmith's brusqueness. Neither of them said much by way of response, but I sensed immediately their concern that a man whom it was clearly hard to take to should be charged with the care of a tragically orphaned child. Already all three of us knew that that felt wrong.

The General walked with the assistance of a cane and always would now. But he walked more easily than he had at first. My neck and my left cheek had healed, and what they'd said was right: make-up effortlessly obscured the tiny fissures. By now Otmar could light his own cigarettes, gripping the matchbox between his knees. He had difficulty with meat, and one of us always cut it up for him. He'd have to learn to type again, but cleverly he managed to play patience. 'Solo?' Aimée would say when a game had been resolved, and after they'd played a few hands she would arrange the draughts on the draughts-board. There was another game, some German game I didn't understand, with torn-up pieces of paper.

The old man told her stories, not about his schooldays but concerning the adventures he'd had as a soldier. They sat together in the inner hall, he in a ladder-backed chair, she on one of my peacock-embroidered stools. He murmured through the quiet of an afternoon while the household rested, a faint scent of floor polish on the air. They chose the inner hall because it's always cool.

As for me, on all those days I stared at the only words I had typed on my green paper since the outrage. I counted them – thirty-six, thirty-eight with the title. Everything that should have followed I was deprived of, and I knew by now that this was the loss I must put beside the greater loss of a girlfriend, and of a daughter, and of a father, a mother and a brother.

The private room set aside for my writing is a brown-shadowed cubicle with heavy curtains that keep both heat and light out, the ornate ivy of its wallpaper simulating a further coolness. Besides the glass-faced cabinet that contains my titles, there is my desk, surfaced in green leather, and a matching chair. Here I sat during those days of June, the cover lifted from my black Olympia, my typing paper mostly blank. I could not glimpse my heroine's face, nor even find her name. Esmeralda? Deborah? I could not find the barest hint of a relationship or the suggestion, however foggy, of a story. There was still only the swish of a white dress, a single moment before that flimsy ghost was gone again.

'Apparently, a scholarly gentleman, this Mr Riversmith,' Quinty remarked one evening after dinner, interrupting my weary efforts by placing a glass of gin and tonic on the desk beside me. 'I don't think I ever met a professor before.'

I hadn't either. I sipped the drink, hoping he'd go away. But Quinty never does what you want him to do.

'The doctor tells me Mr Riversmith's never so much as laid an eye on young Aimée. Did he say the same to you? A rift between the late sister and himself?'

I shook my head. Briskly, I thanked him for bringing me the drink. I hadn't asked him to. One of Quinty's many assumptions is that in such matters he invariably knows best.

'What I'm thinking is, how will the wife welcome a kid she's never so much as laid an eye on either?'

Again I indicated that I did not know. It naturally would not be easy for Mrs Riversmith, I suggested. I didn't imagine she was expecting it to be.

'Interesting type of gentleman,' Quinty remarked. 'Interesting to meet a guy like that.'

He stood there, still tiresome, fiddling with objects on my desk. They'd never find the culprits now, he said; you could forget all that. As soon as Riversmith came for the child the old man and the German would go. That stood to reason; they couldn't stay for ever; the whole thing would be over then. 'You'll pay the German's bill, eh?'

'I said I would.'

He laughed the way he does. 'You'll get your reward in heaven,' he repeated for the umpteenth time in our relationship. A kind of catch-phrase this is with him: he doesn't believe it. What he knows – though it's never spoken between us – is that the house will be his and Rosa Crevelli's when I die. My own reward has nothing to do with anything.

'Roast in hell, the rest of us,' he said before he went away.

Mr Riversmith telephoned again; we had a similar conversation. I reported on his niece's continuing progress, what she had done that day, what she had said. When there was nothing left to say the conversation ended. There was a pause, a cough, the woman's voice in the background, a dismissive word of farewell.

A few days later he telephoned a third time. He'd had further conversations with Dr Innocenti, he said; he suggested a date – a week hence – for his arrival in my house. There was the usual prickly atmosphere, the same empty pause before he brought himself to say goodbye. I poured myself a drink and walked out to the terrace with it. The awkward conversation echoed; I watched the fireflies twinkling in the gloom. How indeed would that woman react to the advent of a child who was totally strange to her? What was the woman like? With someone less cold, the subject of what it was going to be like for both of them might even have been brought up on the telephone. Thomas Riversmith sounded a lot older than his sister. Capricorn, I'd guessed after our first conversation. You often get an uptight Capricorn.

On the terrace I lit a cigarette. Then, quite without warning, monstrously shattering the peaceful evening, the screaming of the child began, the most awful sound I've ever heard.

6

Dr Innocenti came at once. He was calm, and calmly soothed our anxiety. He placed Aimée under temporary sedation, warning us that its effects would not last long. He maintained from the first that there was no need to take her into hospital again, that nothing would be gained. His strength and his tranquillity allowed me to accompany him to the bedside; afterwards he sat with me in the *salotto*, sipping a glass of mineral water. He wished to be within earshot when Aimée emerged from her sleep, since each time she did so she would find herself deeper in what seemed like a nightmare.

'You comprehend, signora? Reversal of waking from bad dreams. For this child such dreams begin then.'

Together we returned to the bedside when the screaming started again, but Dr Innocenti did not administer the drug immediately. Aimée sobbed when the screams had exhausted her, and while she threw her head about on the pillow a dreadful shivering seeming to wrench her small body asunder. I begged him to put a stop to it.

'We understand, Aimée,' he murmured instead, in unhurried tones. 'Here are your friends.'

The child ignored the sympathy. Her eyes stared wide, like those of a creature demented. More sedation was given at last.

'She will sleep till morning now,' the doctor promised, 'and then be drowsy for a little time. I will be here before another crisis.'

From the hall he telephoned Thomas Riversmith to inform

him of the development. 'May I urge you to delay your journey, signore?' I heard him say. 'Three weeks maybe? Four? Not easy now to calculate.'

It was impossible not to have confidence in Dr Innocenti. All his predictions came naturally about, as if he and nature shared some knowledge. There was compassion in the cut of his features, and even in the way he moved, yet it never hindered him. Pity can be an enemy, I know that well.

His presence in my house that night was a marvel. It affected Otmar and the General: without speaking a word, as though anxious only to be co-operative, they went to their rooms and closed their doors. I alone bade the doctor good-night and watched the little red tail-light of his car creeping away into the darkness, still glowing long after the sound of the engine had died.

'Very presentable, the doctor,' Quinty remarked in the hall, even in these wretched circumstances attempting to be jokey or whatever it was he would have called it.

'Yes, very.'

'A different kettle of fish from a certain medical party who had better stay nameless, eh?'

He referred to the doctor who'd been a regular in the Café Rose, a man whose weight was said to be twenty-four stone, whose stomach hung hugely out above the band of his trousers, whose chest was like a woman's. Great sandalled feet shuffled and thumped; like florid blubber, thick lips were loosely open; eyes, piglike, peered. 'We could make a go of it,' was the suggestion he once made to me, and I have no doubt that Quinty knew about this. I have no doubt that the offer was later guffawed over at the card-table.

'I'll say good-night so,' Quinty went on. 'I think it'll be best for all of us when Uncle comes.'

'Good-night, Quinty.'

*

I could not sleep. I could not even close my eyes. I tried not to recall the sound of those screams, that stark, high-pitched shrieking that had chilled me to my very bones. Instead I made myself think about the obese doctor whom Quinty had so conveniently dredged up. You'd never have guessed he was a medical man, more like someone who drilled holes in the street. Yet when an elderly farmer sustained a heart attack in an upstairs room at the café he appeared to know what to do, and there was talk of cures among the natives.

In my continued determination not to dwell on the more immediate past I again saw vividly, as I had on my early-morning walk, the hand of Otmar's girlfriend reaching for the herbs in the supermarket; I saw the General and his well-loved wife. 'I'll get Sergeant Beeds on to you,' Mrs Trice shouted the day she came back early from the laundry. 'Lay another finger on her and you'll find yourself in handcuffs.' The man I'd once taken to be my father blustered and then pleaded, a kind of gibberish coming out of him.

All through that night my mind filled with memories and dreams, a jumble that went on and on, imaginings and reality. 'Please,' Madeleine begged, and Otmar moved his belongings into her flat. When she was out at work he drank a great deal of coffee, and smoked, and typed the articles he submitted to newspapers. Madeleine cooked him moussaka and chicken stew, and once they went to Belgium because he'd heard of an incident which he was convinced would make a newspaper story: how a young man had ingeniously taken the place of a Belgian couple's son after a period of army service.

'So's you can't see up her skirts,' a boy who had something wrong with him said, but no one believed that that was why Miss Alzapiedi wore long dresses. Miss Alzapiedi didn't even know about people looking up skirts. 'If you close your eyes you can *feel* the love of Jesus,' Miss Alzapiedi said. 'Promise me now. Wherever you are, in all your lives, find time to feel the love of Jesus.' Nobody liked the boy who had something wrong with him. When he grinned inanely you had to avert your gaze. The girls pulled his hair whenever he made his rude noise, if Miss Alzapiedi wasn't looking.

'Ah, how d'you do?' the General greeted his would-be son-in-law beneath the tree I'd heard about. The drinks were on a white table among the deck-chairs, Martini already mixed, with ice and lemon, in a tall glass jug. 'So very pleased,' his wife said, and he watched the face of his daughter's fiancé, the features crinkling in a polite acknowledgement, the lips half open. The intimacy of kissing, he thought, damp and sensual. His stomach heaved; he turned away. 'So *very* pleased,' he heard again.

The aviator who wrote messages in the sky wanted to marry me before the obese doctor did. He had retired from the sky-writing business when I knew him, but often he spoke of it in the Café Rose, repeating the message he had a thousand times looped and dotted high above Africa: *Drink Bailey's Beer*. A condition of the inner ear had dictated his retirement, but one day he risked his life and flew again. 'Look, missy!' Poor Boy Abraham cried excitedly, pulling me out of the café on to the dirt expanse where the trucks parked. 'Look! Look!' And there, in the sky, like shaving foam, was my name and an intended compliment. A tiny aircraft, soundless from where we stood, formed the last few letters and then smeared a zigzag flourish. 'Oh, that is *beautiful!*' Poor Boy Abraham cried as we watched. 'Oh, *my*, it's beautiful!' Fortunately Poor Boy Abraham could not read.

'He forgot to lock the windows,' Aimée repeated firmly at the railway station. The Italian woman was angry and almost stamped her foot; the man was smaller than she was, with oiled black hair brushed straight back. 'More likely he left something turned on,' Aimée's brother suggested. 'Maybe the stove.' Aimée disagreed, but then the train came in and they had to find their way to Carrozza 219. When the train moved again Aimée gazed out at the fields of sunflowers, at the green vine shoots in orderly rows and the hot little railway stations. She stared at the pale sky, all the blue bleached out of it. Some of the fields were being sprayed with water that gushed from a jet going round and round. In the far distance there were hills with clumps of trees on them. 'Cypresses,' her father said as the bell of the restaurant attendant tinkled and the businessmen and the fashion woman rose. The woman would have turned off the stove herself, Aimée whispered, and her brother turned grumpily away from her. 'Stop that silly arguing,' their mother reprimanded.

'No, of course I don't mind,' Madeleine said when Otmar asked if his friends might come to the flat when she was out. His friends were intense young men, students or unemployed, one of them a girl whom Madeleine was jealous of. When Otmar and Madeleine were in Italy two of them came up while they were sitting in the sun outside a café. They gave Otmar the name of a cheap restaurant, but afterwards he lost the piece of paper he'd written it down on. 'Look, there're your friends,' Madeleine said a few days later, pointing to where they sat at a café table with two other men, but Otmar didn't want to join them, although they could have given him the name of the restaurant again.

'Rum and Coke,' Ernie Chubbs ordered in the Al Fresco Club, and the Eastern girl brought it quickly, flashy with him as she always was with the customers. They didn't put any rum in mine although Ernie paid for it. They never did in the Al Fresco, saying a girl could end up anywhere if she didn't stay sober. 'Now then, my pretty maid,' Ernie Chubbs said in our corner. I couldn't see his face, I didn't know what it looked like because it was shadowy where we sat and I'd only caught a glimpse of it on the street. 'Often come here, darling?' he chattily questioned me.

Best White Tits in Africa! the writing said in the sky, but in my dream it was different. *Angela Fresu, aged three*, it said, as it does in marble at Bologna.

When I awoke next there was a dusky light in the room. I reached out for a cigarette and lit it, and closed my eyes. 'I shall love you,' Jason says in *For Ever More*, 'till the scent has gone from the flowers and the salt from the seas.' But Jason and Maggie are different from the people I'd kept company with in the night. You can play around with Jason and Maggie, you can change what you wish to change, you can make them do what they're told.

I must digress here. To compose a romance it is necessary to have a set of circumstances and within those circumstances a cast of people. As the main protagonists of a cast, you have, for instance, Jason and Maggie and Maggie's self-centred sister, and Jason's well-to-do Uncle Cedric. The circumstances are that Jason and Maggie want to start a riding stables, but they have very little money. Maggie's sister wants Jason for herself, and Jason's Uncle Cedric will allow the pair a handsome income if Jason agrees to go into the family business, manufacturing girder-rivets. You must also supply places of interest – in this instance the old mill that would make an ideal stables, the little hills over which horses can be exercised, and far away – darkly unprepossessing – the family foundry. You need dramatic incident: the discovery of the machinations of Maggie's sister, the angry family quarrel when Jason refuses to toe his Uncle Cedric's line. None of it's any good if the people aren't real to you as you compose.

In the early morning after that unsettled night it seemed to me that the only story I was being offered was the story of the summer that was slipping by. The circumstances were those that followed a tragedy, the people were those who had crowded my night, the places you can guess. *Ceaseless Tears* was a working title only, and that morning I abandoned it. All

I had dreamed was the chaos from which order was to be drawn, one way or another. Everything in storytelling, romantic or otherwise, is hit and miss, and the fact that reality was involved didn't appear to make much difference.

I prayed, and then I finished my cigarette and soon afterwards rose. I walked about my house in the cool of the morning, relishing its tranquillity and the almost eerie feeling that possessed me: inspiration, or whatever you care to call it, had never before struck me in so strange a manner. I poured myself some tonic water and added just a trace of the other to pep it up. It seemed like obtuseness that I hadn't realized the girl in the white dress was Aimée.

7

Aimée was calm when she awoke, but during the days that followed there were further setbacks, though thankfully none was as alarming as the first one. Her uncle's departure from America was again delayed to allow her further time to make a recovery. But even so Dr Innocenti was optimistic.

We ourselves – the General, Otmar and I – were naturally apprehensive and each day that ended without incident seemed like a victory of a kind. And for me there was another small source of pleasure, a bolt from the blue as agreeable as any I have experienced. As I recall it now I am reminded, by way of introduction, that overheard conversations do not always throw up welcome truths. 'Pass on, my dear, for you'll hear no good,' Lady Daysmith advises in *Precious September*, but of course it is not always so. Pausing by the door of the *salotto* one evening, I overheard Otmar and the General tentatively conversing.

'Yes, she has mentioned that,' the old man was saying, and this was when I paused, for I sensed it was I who was referred to, and who can resist a moment's listening in such circumstances?

'I would take the chance,' Otmar said, 'to pay my debt to her.'

His wife had been quite expert, the old man said next, especially where the cultivation of fritillaries was concerned. Otmar didn't understand the term; an explanation followed, the plant described. The name came from the Latin: *fritıllus* meant a dice-box. 'She was always interested in a horticultural derivation. She read Dr Linnaeus.'

Otmar professing ignorance again, there came an explanation. I heard that this Linnaeus, a Swedish person apparently – Linné as he'd been born – had sorted out a whole array of flowers and plants, giving them names or finding Latin roots for existing names, orderliness and Latin being his forte.

'She wants a garden,' Otmar said, not interrupting but by the sound of it repeating what he had said already, in an effort to bring the conversation down to earth.

'Then we must make her one.'

How could they make me a garden? One was too old, the other had but a single arm left! Yet how sweet it was to hear them! As I stood there I felt a throb of warmth within my body, as though a man had said when I was still a girl: 'I love you . . .'

'He's not the sort of person,' the old man was observing when next I paid attention. 'He's not the sort to be a help or even be much interested.'

I guessed they spoke of Quinty, and certainly what was deduced was true.

'A machine is there?' Otmar asked then. 'An implement to break the earth?'

'There's a thing in England called a Merry Tiller. A motorized plough.'

I imagine Otmar nodded. The General said:

'Heaven knows what grows best in such dry conditions. Precious little, probably. We'd have to read all that up.'

'I do not know seeds.'

Fuchsias grew in the garden of his parents, Otmar went on. He was not good about the names of plants, but he remembered fuchsias in pots – double headed, scarlet and cream. The geranium family should do well, the General said, and brooms. To my delight he mentioned azaleas. Shade would be important, and would somehow have to be supplied. The azaleas would have to be grown in urns, and moved inside in winter.

'With one arm,' Otmar reminded him, 'I could not dig.'

'It is remarkable what can be done, you know. Once you settle to it.'

I moved away because I heard them get to their feet. A few minutes later I saw them at the back of my house, gesturing to one another beside the ruined out-buildings. Their voices drifted to where I watched from; the old man pointed. Here there'd be a flight of steps, leading to a lower level, here four flowerbeds formally in a semi-circle, here a marble figure perhaps. A few days later, when they revealed their secret to me, they showed me the plans they had drawn on several sheets of paper in the meantime. The General promised a herb bed, with thyme and basil and tarragon and rosemary. There would be solitary yew trees or local pines, whichever were advised. They'd try for box hedges and cotoneaster and oleander. There'd be a smoke tree and a handkerchief tree, and roses and peach trees, whatever they could induce to thrive.

'When I'm grown up I'd like to tell stories too.'

Aimée had *Flight to Enchantment* in her hand. She had asked me and I had related its contents, while effortlessly she listened.

'I like being here in the hills,' she said.

8

On 14 July Thomas Riversmith arrived. Telephoning a few evenings before, he insisted that he did not wish to be met; that he wished to cause the minimum of inconvenience. So he took a taxi from Pisa, which is an extremely long journey, and then there was difficulty finding my house. From an upstairs window I watched him paying his driver in one-hundred-thousand-lire notes. He had black Mandarina Duck bags. I went downstairs, to welcome him in the inner hall.

He was a tall, thickset man, rather heavy about the face, not at all like the young woman on the train. His eyes, between beetle-black brows, were opaque – green or blue, it wasn't apparent which; his crinkly hair was greyish. Mr Riversmith was indeed as serious and as solemn as he had seemed on the telephone: the surprise was that, in his way, he was a handsome man. He wore a dark suit, which had become creased on his air flight and creased again due to his sitting in a hired car for so long. His wife would have bought him the Mandarina luggage; it didn't match the rest of him in any way whatsoever.

'I'm Mrs Delahunty.'

He nodded, not saying who he was because no doubt he assumed that no one else was expected just then. He stood there, not seeming interested in anything, waiting for me to say something else. It was a little after six in the evening; the cocktail hour, as the Americans call it. A certain weariness about his features intimated that Mr Riversmith could do with a drink.

'Drink?' he repeated when I suggested this. He shook his head. He had better wash, he said. He had a way of looking at you intently when he spoke, while giving the impression that he didn't see you. Beneath the scrutiny I felt foolish, the way you do with some people.

'Quinty'll take you up, Mr Riversmith.'

'After that I should see my niece.'

'Of course. Simply when you're ready, Mr Riversmith, please join us in the *salotto*.'

He followed Quinty upstairs. I made my way to my private room. Earlier in the day an accumulation of fan mail had come, forwarded from the publisher's offices in London. After that brief encounter with Mr Riversmith I found it something of an antidote. People endeavour to explain how much a story means to them, or how they identify. *I quite felt I was Rosalind. Years ago, of course. I'm in my eighties now.* Occasionally a small gift is enclosed, a papier mâché puzzle from Japan, a pressed flower, inexpensive jewellery. *Was Lucinda* really *furious or just pretending? Will Mark forgive her, utterly and completely? Oh, I do so hope he can!* Little adhesive labels come, for autographs. *I have all your stories, but dare not trust them to the post. Return postage enclosed.* I do my best to reply, aptly, but sometimes become exhausted, faced with so much. *What a lovely birthday party Ms Penny Court had! It reminded me so much of my own when I was twenty-one and Dad made a key out of plaster of Paris and silver paint! I'm forty now, with kiddies of my own and Alec (husband) is no longer here so I do my best on my own. I always think of her as Ms Penny Court, I don't know why. I envy her her independence. Dad and I were close, that's why he made the key for my twenty-first, you remember things like that. I'm fond of the kiddies of course, it goes without saying, and they wouldn't be here if I hadn't married Alec. He went off two years ago, a woman security officer.* Often the letters go on for many pages, the ink changing colour more than once, the writing-paper acquiring stains. When gifts of food are sent I am naturally touched, but I throw the food away, having been warned that this is advisable.

Dear Ron, I wrote on the evening of Thomas Riversmith's arrival, addressing my correspondent so familiarly because I'd been supplied with that name only. *Thank you for your nice letter. I am glad you enjoyed 'More than the Brave.' It is interesting what you say about Annabella and Roger being acquainted in a previous life. I quite accept this may be so, and I am interested in what you tell me about your pets. I do not believe your wife would be in the least aggrieved to know you find Fred a comfort. In fact, I'm sure she's delighted.* I added another sentence about the ferret, Fred, then placed the letter in an envelope and sealed it. I never supply strangers with my address, having been warned that this is inadvisable also. And some correspondents I really do have to ignore. Correspondence with the disturbed is not a good idea.

Mr Riversmith was standing in silence in the *salotto* when I entered.

'Would I mix you a drink, sir?' Quinty offered.

'A drink?'

'Would you care for a refreshment after your journey, sir?'

Mr Riversmith requested an Old Fashioned, then noticed my presence and addressed me. He remarked that his niece was pretty.

'Yes, indeed.' But I added that Aimée was still mentally fragile. I said that Dr Innocenti would visit us in the morning. He would explain about that.

'I greatly appreciate what Dr Innocenti has done for my niece.' Mr Riversmith paused. 'And I appreciate your looking after her in her convalescence, Mrs Delahunty.'

I explained about the tourists who stayed in my house when the hotels were full. It was no trouble was how I put it; we were used to visitors.

'You'll let me have an account?' Mr Riversmith went on, as if anxious to deal with all the formalities at once. 'I would wish to have that in order before we leave.'

I said that was Quinty's department, and Quinty nodded as he handed Mr Riversmith his glass. 'G and t would it be tonight?' he murmured. He rolls that 'g and t' off his tongue in a twinkling manner, appearing to take pleasure in the sound, heaven knows why.

'Thank you, Quinty,' I said, and as I spoke the General entered the room.

I introduced the two men, revealing in lowered tones that the General had been only a couple of seats away from Aimée on the train. I mentioned Otmar in case Mr Riversmith had forgotten what I'd said on the telephone. Lowering my voice further, I mentioned the old man's daughter and son-in-law, and Madeleine. In the circumstances I considered that necessary.

'You've come for the child,' the General said.

'Yes, I have.'

There was a silence. Quinty poured the General some whisky, and noted the drinks in the little red notebook he keeps by the tray of bottles. The old man nodded, acknowledging what had been said. In order to ease a certain stickiness that had developed I asked a question to which I knew the answer. 'You do not know Aimée well?' I remarked to Mr Riversmith.

'I met my niece for the first time in my life half an hour ago.'

'What?' The General frowned. 'What?' he said again.

'I never knew either of my sister's children.' He appeared not to wish to say anything more, to leave the matter there.

But then, unexpectedly, he added what I knew also: that there'd been a family quarrel.

'So the child's a stranger to you?' the General persisted. 'And you to her?'

'That is so.'

His wife would have accompanied him, Mr Riversmith continued, apropos of another question the General asked, but unfortunately it had been impossible for her to get away. He referred to his wife as Francine, a name new to me. In answer to a question of my own he supplied the information that his wife was in the academic world also.

'We should be calling you professor,' I put in. 'We weren't entirely certain.'

He replied that he didn't much use the title. Academic distinctions were unimportant, he said. The General asked him what his line of scholarship was, and Mr Riversmith replied – his tone unchanged – that the bark-ant was his subject. He spoke of this insect as if it were a creature as familiar to us as the horse or the dog.

The General shook his head. He did not know the bark-ant, he confessed. Mr Riversmith made a very slight, scarcely perceptible shrugging motion. The interdependency of bark-ant colonies in acacia trees, he stated, revealed behaviour that was similar to human beings'. It was an esoteric area of research where the layman was concerned, he admitted in the end, and changed the subject.

'My niece will not forget the time she's spent here.'

'No, she'll hardly do that,' the General agreed.

Otmar came in, his hand grasping one of Aimée's. I introduced him to Mr Riversmith, and I thought for a moment that he might click his heels, for Otmar's manner can be formal on occasion. But he only bowed. Quinty, still hovering near the drinks' tray, poured Aimée a Coca-Cola and Otmar a Stella Artois. He made the entries in the notebook and then sloped away.

'Those are interesting pictures you drew,' Aimée's uncle said.

'Which pictures?'

'The ones on your walls.'

'I didn't draw them.'

'I drew the pictures,' Otmar said.

'Otmar drew them,' Aimée said.

For the first time Mr Riversmith was taken aback. I knew that Dr Innocenti would already have spoken to him on the telephone about the pictures. I watched him wondering if he'd misunderstood what he'd been told. He opened his mouth to speak, but Aimée interrupted.

'When are you taking me away?'

'We'll see what Dr Innocenti says when he comes tomorrow.'

'I'm better.'

'Of course you are.'

'Really better.'

Aimée, in a plain red dress that she and Signora Bardini had bought together, took up a position in the centre of the room. Otmar leaned against the pillar of an archway. The fear was still in his eyes, but it had calmed a little.

'Feel like that long journey soon?' Mr Riversmith was asking Aimée in the artificial voice some people put on for children. 'Tiring, you know, being up in the air like that.'

'You want to rest?' She stumbled slightly over the words, and then repeated them. 'You want to rest, Uncle?'

'It's just that we mustn't hurry your uncle,' I quietly interjected. 'He needs a little breathing space before turning round to go all that way back again.'

The conversation became ordinary then, the General in his courteous way continuing to ask our visitor the conventional questions that such an occasion calls for: where it was he lived in the United States, if he had children of his own? You'd never have guessed from the way he kept the chat going with Mr Riversmith that the General's courage had deserted him, that he could not bring himself to visit an empty house or even to expose himself to the talk of solicitors.

'Virginsville,' Mr Riversmith responded, giving the name of the town where he resided. 'Pennsylvania.'

He supplied the name of the nearby university where he conducted his research with the creatures he'd mentioned. I was right in my surmise that no children had been born to Francine and himself.

'Nor to my daughter,' the General said.

In response to further politeness, Mr Riversmith revealed that his wife had children, now grown up, by a previous marriage. I asked if he'd been married before himself, and he said he had. Then he went silent again, and the General saved the situation by telling him about the garden that was planned. In a corner Otmar and Aimée were whispering together, playing their game with torn-up pieces of paper. The General mentioned the names of various plants – moss phlox, I remember, and *magnolia campbellii*. He wondered if tree peonies, another favourite of his wife's, would thrive in Umbrian soil. Trial and error he supposed it would have to be. Enthusiastically, he added that Quinty had discovered a motorized plough could be hired locally, with a man to operate it.

'I have little knowledge of horticultural matters,' Mr Riversmith stated.

As he spoke, for some reason I imagined 5 May in Virginsville, Pennsylvania. I imagined Mr Riversmith entering his residence, and Francine saying: 'One of those bomb attacks in Italy.' Easily, still, I visualize that scene. She is drinking orange juice. On the television screen there is a wrecked train. 'How was your day?' she asks when he has embraced her, as mechanically as he always does when he returns from his day's research. 'Oh, it was adequate,' he replies. (I'm certain he chose that word.) 'They're colonizing quite remarkably at the moment.' *Her* day has been exhausting, Francine says. She had difficulty with the hood of the Toyota, which jammed again, the way it has been doing lately. No terrorist group claimed responsibility, the television newscaster is saying.

'Does your wife research into ants too, Mr Riversmith?' I asked because another lull hung heavily and because, just then, I felt curious.

Before he replied he drew his lips together – stifling a sigh, it might have been, or some kind of nervous twitch. 'My wife shares my discipline,' he managed eventually. 'Yes, that is so.'

Weeks later, it would have been the local police in Virginsville who supplied the information that those television pictures concerned him more than either he or Francine had thought. That scene came clearly to me also, still does: the officers declining to sit down, sunlight glittering on their metal badges. 'Italy?' The staccato tightness of Thomas Riversmith's voice seems strained to the policemen, and even to himself. 'The little girl's out of hospital, sir,' one of the men informs him. 'She's being looked after in a local house.' Still numbed, Mr Riversmith mumbles questions. Why had the explosion occurred? Had it in any way to do with Americans being on the train? Had those responsible been apprehended? 'My God!' Francine exclaims, entering the room just then. 'My *God!*'

We had dinner on the terrace. Mr Riversmith stirred himself and with an effort admired the view.

The next morning Dr Innocenti went through for Mr Riversmith his lengthy account of Aimée's progress. From the doctor's tone and from Mr Riversmith's responses, it was clear that much of what had already been said on the telephone was being repeated. Patiently, Dr Innocenti confirmed and elucidated, expanding when he considered it necessary. In the end he said he saw no reason why the return journey should not be made as soon as Mr Riversmith felt ready for it. He himself had done all he could for the child. Making what for him was quite a little speech, Mr Riversmith thanked him.

'One thing I'd like to raise, doctor. Aimée insists she didn't paint those pictures.'

'She doesn't know she did, signore.'

'The German – '

'It's good that Otmar helps.'

'Aimée and Otmar have become friends,' I said.

Mr Riversmith frowned. Impatience flitted through his features. It was that, I realized then, that made him seem cross from time to time. Impatience was his problem, not nerves. He held his seriousness to him, as though protectively, as though to cover his impatience. But sometimes it was not up to the task and a kind of irritated fustiness resulted.

'*Non importa, signore,*' Dr Innocenti assured him. 'The pictures are only pictures. Colour on paper.'

'Mr Riversmith does not perhaps understand,' I suggested, 'because he has not observed his niece's recovery.'

'Yes,' Dr Innocenti agreed. For once uncharacteristically vague, he added: 'We must hope.'

That afternoon Mr Riversmith wrote the necessary cheques, for the hospital and for Dr Innocenti. He made arrangements for a gravestone, and paid for it in advance.

Then there was an unexpected development. In one of his many conversations with Aimée Dr Innocenti had described to her the city of Siena, of which he is a native. He had called it the proudest of all Italian cities, full of mysterious corners, sombre and startling in turn: before she returned to America she must certainly visit it. 'You haven't yet?' he'd chided her in mock disappointment that morning. 'Won't you please your old friend, Aimée?'

Later Otmar brought the subject up in the *salotto*. Aimée

had promised Dr Innocenti, he reported, but was too shy to ask.

'Siena?' her uncle said.

It wasn't far, I explained. An excursion could easily be arranged. 'It's a pity not to visit Siena.'

Quinty would drive us. The General would accompany us in the hope of purchasing some gardening books that Quinty might translate for him.

'Would you object to an early start,' I questioned Mr Riversmith, 'in order to avoid the worst of the heat?'

He agreed quite readily to that, though briefly, without elaborating on his sleeping habits as another person might. I couldn't help wondering if Francine was like that too.

'Quinty'll wake you with a cup of tea at half-past six.' I lowered my voice and glanced about me, for this was something I didn't wish the others to overhear. It would be the first time we had all done something together, I confided. 'Since the outrage we haven't had the confidence for much.'

I don't know whether Mr Riversmith heard or not. He simply looked at me, and again I had the impression that he stifled a sigh. It surprised me that Francine, or his previous wife, hadn't ever told him that this habit of his seemed rude.

9

Soon after seven the next morning I observed the General pointing out to Mr Riversmith the features of the motor-car that Quinty has a habit of referring to as his, although, of course, it belongs to me. The old man drew attention to the huge headlights, the chromium fastenings of the luggage-box and of the canvas hood, now folded down. I heard him say that motor-cars were no longer manufactured with such panache and pride. Mr Riversmith no doubt considered it antique. He said something I did not catch.

I had chosen for our excursion a wide-brimmed white hat and a plain white dress, with black and white high-heeled shoes, black belt and handbag. On the gravel expanse in front of my house I greeted the two men, and in a moment Otmar and Aimée appeared, Aimée in the red dress she'd been wearing the evening her uncle arrived. To my amazement, Rosa Crevelli came out of the house also, clearly attired for the outing, in a flowered green outfit with lacy green stockings to match.

'Look here,' I began, drawing Quinty aside, but he interrupted before I'd even mentioned the girl's name.

'You agreed it was OK,' he said. 'When we asked you last night you said the more the merrier.'

'I said no such thing, Quinty.'

'You did, you know. I remarked it would make an outing for the girl. I remarked she was looking peaky these days.'

I firmly shook my head. No such conversation had taken place.

'You had a drink in at the time, signora.'

'Quinty – '

'I'm sorry.'

He hung his head the way only Quinty can do. He protested that neither he nor the girl would offend me for the world; he'd maybe misheard when he thought I'd said the more the merrier.

'You're coming with us in order to drive the car,' I pointed out. 'It's different altogether for a maid to tag along. There's neither rhyme nor reason in it.'

'It's only I promised her when you said that last night. She said you were kindness itself.'

This spoiled everything. I'd so much wanted things to go nicely. I'd wanted it to be a pleasant day for Aimée and her uncle; I'd wanted to get to know Mr Riversmith better; I'd wanted the General and Otmar to go on pulling themselves together, benefiting from the diversion; I'd wanted everyone to begin to be happy again.

'It's peculiar, Quinty, for a maid to mix with house-guests.'

'I know. I know. We're servant class. All I'm saying is, since the misunderstanding is there let it stay. It would be a terrible disappointment for the poor creature. She was ironing her clothes till the small hours.'

So in the end I gave in, even though I felt acutely embarrassed. I resolved to apologize to our guests – well, at least to Mr Riversmith and the General – when a suitable moment arrived. I am servant class myself, as Quinty well knows, but with everyone waiting I didn't want to explain that naturally there was a difference.

'Sorry,' he said again.

I did no more than shake my head at him. Rosa Crevelli had been watching us, gauging the content of our exchanges. I saw him glance at her, and the pout that was just beginning to disturb her sallow features turned into a smile. I approached the others and quietly suggested that Aimée and the maid should occupy the two rear seats, which are a feature of the car, the long middle one folding forward to allow access. Otmar, Mr Riversmith and I occupied this centre section, the General sat with Quinty in the front.

'*Andiamo!*' Quinty exclaimed as he engaged the gears, his sombre mood of a moment ago quite vanished. 'We're on the off!'

The sky was empty of clouds. The morning air was cool and fresh. As we drove, I pointed out distant hill-towns and avenues of cypresses for Mr Riversmith's benefit. Sometimes I indicated a church or, if none loomed near, a roadside café or a petrol station, knowing that for the stranger everything is of interest. Mr Riversmith nodded an acknowledgement from time to time, appearing otherwise to be mulling over matters he did not share. 'Magnificent, this car,' I heard the General say. Now and again Otmar turned round to exchange a word with Aimée.

'You may find it strange,' I remarked to Mr Riversmith, for what I had touched upon the day before had been on my mind in the night, 'that we should be going out on a jaunt while still in the grip of the horror that has torn our lives asunder.'

He shook his head. In a conventional manner he said it was a sign of healing and recovery.

'We long to escape our brooding, Mr Riversmith. We stitch together any kind of surface. But when we look into our hearts we see only a grief that is unbearable.'

I chose those words carefully, and did not add that the loss I'd suffered myself had been far less than that of the others because I'd had far less to lose. I didn't go into detail because it wasn't the time to do so. All I wished to make clear was that when, today, he observed his niece and Otmar and the old Englishman he was observing a skin drawn over human debris. Mr Riversmith said he wouldn't put it quite like that, but didn't offer an alternative form of words.

'I just thought I'd mention it,' I said, and left it at that. The debris of our times, I might have added, but I did not do so.

When we reached Siena, Quinty parked just inside the city gates, positioning the car beneath a tree to keep it cool. When he had raised the canvas roof and locked it into place we set off to walk to the café in the Piazza del Campo, where we were to breakfast. It was quite chilly in the narrow streets we passed through.

'I must apologize,' I murmured in a private moment to Mr Riversmith.

'I beg your pardon?'

I smiled, indicating Rosa Crevelli's presence with a sideways glance. There is something of the gypsy in Rosa Crevelli, which was considerably emphasized by the vivid green of her dress and her lacy stockings.

'I beg your pardon?' Mr Riversmith repeated.

I said it didn't matter because the moment had passed and we could now be overheard. He said yes when I asked him if his wife would care for this city, if the grey alleys in which its natives moved like early-morning ghosts would impress her. When finally we reached our destination the contrast was startling: a bright blaze of sunshine was already baking the paving-stones and terracotta of the elegant, shell-shaped concavity that is the city's centre. Would that, I wondered, impress Mrs Riversmith also?

He didn't reply directly. In fact, strictly speaking, he didn't reply to my question at all. 'Dr Innocenti gave my niece this guide-book,' was what he said, and handed the volume to me, unopened.

The great tower of the city-hall rises imperiously to claim a dominance against the plain serenity of the sky. I glanced through the guide-book when we'd settled ourselves at a table in the shade of the café's awning. Chattering in Italian, Quinty and Rosa Crevelli shook the waiter's hand. Noisily they ordered coffee and brioches. 'The journey's perked her up,' Quinty whispered when he saw me looking at them.

'This is very pleasant,' the General said.

'Yes, indeed,' Mr Riversmith agreed, somewhat to my surprise since he had been so taciturn on the walk from the car.

When the coffee came I drew his attention to an entry in the guide-book about the Palio – the horse-race that takes place each summer through the streets of Siena and around the slopes of the Campo where we now sat. I read the entry aloud: that the race was an occasion coloured by feuds and sharp practice, by the vested interests of other cities and the jealousies of local families, that it was wild and dangerous.

'You'll notice the decorated lamp standards,' Quinty interrupted. 'Tarted up for the big day.'

I wore my dark glasses, and from behind their protection I observed my companions while Quinty continued for a moment about the lamp standards, prompted in what he was saying by the maid. I observed the nervous movement of Otmar's fingers and the twitch of anxiety that caused him often to glance over his shoulder, as if he distrusted his surroundings. The old man's masking of his anguish remained meticulously intact. Aimée examined the pictures on the little sachets of sugar that had come with our coffee.

'The Sienese are renowned for the macaroons they bake,' I remarked to Mr Riversmith. 'Those *ricciarelli* we have at tea-time.'

'Yes,' he said.

Later, on the way to the cathedral, we called in at a travel agency, where he confirmed with the clerk the details of the flight back to Pennsylvania. The booking was made for four days' time, I myself gently pressing that Mr Riversmith should allow his jet-lag to ease before rushing off. 'I expect you've thought about how Aimée'll settle with you,' I said when these formalities were completed and we were on the street again. 'You and your wife.'

Again there was the tightening of the lips, the sharp, swift nod, another silence.

'Tell me about your sister,' I invited, tentatively, as we moved on.

Before I'd finished speaking Mr Riversmith stopped in his walk. He turned to me in a deliberate way and said that every time he looked at Aimée he was reminded of his sister. Aimée had Phyl's hair and her eyes and her freckles. I said yes, I knew, but the observation was ignored. Then, to my astonishment, while still standing on the street, the others now far ahead of us in their climb to the cathedral, Mr Riversmith related the history of the family trouble there had been. His sister had been particularly fond of his first wife. His second, the one called Francine, had somehow discovered this, had even learnt of Phyl's repeated endeavours to bring the two together again. A couple of months after he married Francine she and Phyl quarrelled so violently that they had avoided speaking to one another since. He had taken Francine's side and Phyl hadn't forgiven him. The ugly breach that followed accounted for the fact that her children were unknown to him; he remembered his brother-in-law Jack only from the single occasion he'd met him. A dozen times Mr Riversmith had apparently been on the point of writing to Phyl to see if amends might be made. But he had never done so.

'Naturally, I was apprehensive, coming out here,' Mr Riversmith confessed. 'I'd never even seen a photograph of my niece.'

All the fustiness had gone from him. For the first time he appeared to be a normal human person, endeavouring to contribute to a conversation. He was not a loquacious man; no circumstances in the world would ever alter that. Yet this moving little account of family troubles had tumbled out of him in the most natural way – hesitantly and awkwardly, it's true, but none the less naturally. I was aware of a pleasant sensation in my head, like faint pins-and-needles, and a pleasant warmth in my body. My first concern was to throw the ball back.

'Aimée didn't know she had an uncle,' I pointed out. 'So if you and Francine imagine you were condemned in her eyes by your sister that wouldn't be correct.'

He appeared to be taken aback by that. He even gave a little jump.

'Of course you weren't condemned,' I repeated. 'Your sister had a generous face.'

He didn't comment on the observation. I asked when he'd last seen his sister and he said at their mother's funeral.

'A long time ago?'

'1975.'

'And your father? Yours and Phyl's?'

Again there was surprise. The father had died when Phyl was an infant, and I imagined the household that was left, he taking the father's place, much older than the sister. I imagined him mending things about the house the way his father had, cultivating lettuces and eggplant. I wondered if Phyl had thought the world of him, as younger sisters in such circumstances often do.

'Don't feel guilty,' I begged, and told him how the General hadn't been able to respect his son-in-law and could not find the courage to walk into an empty house or even to cope with solicitors – he whom courage had so characterized. I mentioned Otmar's Madeleine.

While I was speaking I recalled a dream I'd had the night before. At once I wished to recount it, the way one does, but Mr Riversmith being the man he was, I found myself unable to do so. As you've probably deduced by now, dreams have a fascination for me. The Austrian ivory cutter – and, come to that, Poor Boy Abraham – used regularly to seek me out in order to retail a dream, and occasionally I would pass on what I'd dreamed myself. This one, in fact, concerned Mr Riversmith and might indeed have interested him, but still I felt inhibited. In it he was a younger man, little more than a boy. He was repairing a kitchen drawer that had fallen to pieces in Phyl's hands, the sides dropping away from one another as if the glue that held them had become defective. He scraped away a kind of fungus from the joints and placed the drawer in clamps, with fresh glue replacing the old. 'You're clever to do that,' Phyl said, and the wooden slat of the kitchen blind tapped the window-frame, the way it did in even the slightest breeze when the window was half open. I longed to ask him about that as we climbed the hill to the cathedral, but still I held my peace.

The others were by now out of sight. We found them waiting for us on the cathedral steps, and with Dr Innocenti's guide-book open the General led the way into the wasp-like building, reading aloud about the floor and the carved pulpit. When we had exhausted the marvels of this most impressive place and had visited the little museum near by, we made for the picture gallery proper. To my considerable relief, Quinty and Rosa Crevelli had disappeared.

In the quiet of the gallery I would have liked to pursue my conversation with Mr Riversmith, but as we made the rounds of the pictures he fell into step with Otmar and the General, leaving me for the moment on my own. Aimée had wandered on ahead.

'Look at this!' I heard her cry in another room, and a moment later we were all congregated around the painting that excited her.

It was called *Annuncio ai pastori*, and depicted two shepherds and a rat-like dog crouched by a fire that had been kindled beside carefully penned sheep. The hills around about were the hills of Italy turned into a brown desert, the sky an Italian sky, and the buildings in the background and the foreground were of Italian architecture. But an angel, holding out a sprig of something, was floating in a glow of yellow light, and didn't, to my untutored eye, seem quite to belong.

'I've never seen a picture as beautiful,' Aimée said.

It occurred to me, as she spoke, that had the outrage not happened, she would probably have come to this city with her parents and her brother. They would probably have stood in front of this very picture. I looked at her, but her face was radiant. I edged closer to Mr Riversmith, hoping to share this thought with him in a quiet whisper, but unfortunately just as I did so he moved away.

'Look at how the sheep are fenced,' she said. 'Like with a net.'

'Sano di Pietro was born in Siena in 1406 and died in 1481,' the General read from Dr Innocenti's guide-book, and then explained that this was the person who had painted the picture.

'More than five hundred years ago,' I pointed out to Aimée, thinking that would interest her.

'Eight trees,' she counted. 'Eight and a half you *could* say. Nineteen sheep maybe. Or twenty, I guess. It's hard to make them out.'

'More like twenty,' the General estimated.

It was difficult to count them because the shapes ran into one another when two sheep of the same colour were close together. The guide-book, so the General said, suggested that the dog had noticed the angel before the shepherds had. To me that seemed somewhat fanciful, but I didn't say so.

'I love the dog,' Aimée said. 'I *love* it.'

Otmar, who had wandered off to examine other pictures, rejoined us now. Aimée took his hand and pointed out all the features she'd enthused over already. '*Especially* the dog,' she added.

I was quite glad when eventually we descended the stairs

again. Pictures of angels and saints, and the Virgin with the baby Jesus, are very pretty and are of course to be delighted in, but one after another can be too much of a good thing. I wondered if Mr Riversmith's wife would have agreed and, since I very much wanted to establish what this woman was like, I raised the subject with him. I said I had counted more than thirty Virgins.

'The cathedral would perhaps be more Francine's kind of thing?'

But Mr Riversmith was buying a postcard at the time and didn't hear. It was interesting that he'd been married twice. I wondered about that, too.

'Otmar says you can climb up the town-hall tower,' Aimée said in the postcards place. 'We're going to.'

On the way back to the Piazza del Campo I noticed Quinty and Rosa Crevelli loitering in a doorway. They were smoking and leafing through a photographic magazine, giggling as Quinty turned the pages. I was glad they didn't see us and that no one happened to be looking in their direction as we went by. You could tell by the cover the kind of magazine it was.

'Why didn't I ever see you?' I heard Aimée ask her uncle. 'I didn't even know I *had* an uncle.'

I didn't catch his reply, something about the distance between Virginsville, Pennsylvania, and wherever it was she and her family had lived. Clearly he didn't want to go into it all, but as we turned into the piazza she still persisted, appearing to know something of the truth.

'Didn't you like her?'

'I liked her very much.'

'Did you have a fight?'

He hesitated. Then he said:

'A silly disagreement.'

The old man remarked that he would not ascend the tower but instead would search for his gardening manuals. We made an arrangement to meet in an hour's time at the restaurant next to the café where we'd had breakfast, Il Campo. I went off on my own, to look in the shoe shops.

I was after a pair of tan mid-heels, but I wasn't successful in my search so I slipped into a bar near that square with all the banks in it. '*Ecco, signora!*' the waiter jollily exclaimed, bringing me what I ordered. It was pleasant sitting there, watching the people. A smartly dressed couple sat near me, the woman subtly made up, her companion elegant in a linen suit, with a blue silk tie. A lone man, bearded, read *La Stampa*. Two pretty girls, like twins, gossiped. '*Ecco, signora!*' the waiter said again. It was extraordinary, the dream I'd had about Mr Riversmith, and I kept wondering how on earth I could have come to have such knowledge of anything as private as that, and in such telling detail. I kept hearing his voice telling me about the family dispute, and I rejoiced that we had at last conversed.

'*Bellissima!*' a salesgirl enthused a little later. I held between my hands a brightly coloured hen. I had noticed it in a window full of paper goods, side by side with a strikingly coiled serpent and a crocodile. Each was a mass of swirling, jagged colours on what from a distance I took to be papier mâché. But when I handled the animals I discovered they were of carved wood, with paper pressed over the surface instead of paint.

I bought the hen because it was the most amusing. It was wrapped for me in black tissue paper and placed in a carrier-bag with a design of footprints on it. Did he love Francine? I wondered, and again I tried to visualize her – inspecting insects through a microscope, driving her Toyota. But I did not succeed.

Instead, as I left the shop, I saw Mr Riversmith himself. He was turning a corner and disappeared from view while I watched. I paused for a moment, but in the end I hurried after him.

'Mr Riversmith!'

He turned and, when he saw who it was, waited. The street we were in was no more than an alley, sunless and dank. If we turned left at the end of it, Mr Riversmith said, we would soon find ourselves in the Campo again.

'Let's not,' I suggested, perhaps a little daringly.

I had noticed, through a courtyard, a small, pretty hotel with creeper growing all over it. I drew Mr Riversmith towards it.

'This is what we're after.' I guided him through the entrance and into a pleasant bar.

'Are the others coming here? I thought we arranged – '

'Let's just sit down, shall we?'

Imagine a faintly gloomy interior, light obscured by the creeper that trails around the windows. The table-tops are green, chairs and wall-coverings red. The two barmen look like brothers, young and slight, with dark moustaches. Only a sprinkling of other customers occupy tables. There are flowers in vases.

'Are they coming here?' Mr Riversmith asked again.

'A little peace for you,' I replied, smiling friendlily. 'I think you'd welcome a bit of peace and quiet, eh? Now, I insist on standing you a cocktail.'

He shook his head. He said something about not drinking in the middle of the day, but recognizing that this was a polite reluctance to accept more hospitality I ignored it. I ordered him an Old Fashioned, since in my house that had been established as his drink.

'It's awfully pleasant here,' I remarked, smiling again in an effort to make him feel at ease. I said there was no reason why he and I shouldn't be a little late for lunch. If tongues wagged it would be nonsense.

He frowned, as if bewildered by this vernacular expression. I shook my head, indicating that it didn't matter, that nothing of any import had been said. The barman brought our drinks. I said:

'I wonder what sort of a person Sano di Pietro was.'

'Who?'

'The artist who painted the picture the child was so taken with. Incidentally, I thought it was a bit extravagant, that remark in the guide-book about the dog noticing the angel first.'

He appeared to nod, but the movement was so slight I might have been mistaken.

'You thought so too? You noticed that?'

'Well, no, I really can't say I did.'

The place filled up. I drew Mr Riversmith's attention to an elderly man with tiny rimless spectacles in the company of a young girl. Lowering my voice, I asked him what he thought the relationship was. He replied, blankly, that he didn't know.

I asked him about other couples, about a group of men who clearly had some business interest in common. I was reminded of the men in Carrozza 219, but I considered it inappropriate to mention this. One of the group repeatedly took small objects from one of his pockets and placed them for a few moments on the table. I thought they might be buttons. I wondered if the men were in the button business.

'Buttons?' Mr Riversmith said.

'Just a notion,' I said, and then a Japanese party entered the bar and I said that there was one most noticeable thing about the Japanese – you could never guess a thing about them.

'Yes,' Mr Riversmith said.

I kept wanting to reach across the table and touch the back of his hand to reassure him, but naturally I didn't. 'What's the matter?' I wanted to ask him, simply, without being fussy with the question. He didn't offer to buy a drink, which was a pity, because for a man like Mr Riversmith the second drink can be a great loosener. All that sense of communication there'd been when he'd talked about his sister a couple of hours ago had gone.

'I really think we should join the others, Mrs Delahunty.'

Although I'd said it was to be my treat, he had already placed a note on the table and within a few minutes we were back on the street again. I had to hurry to keep up with him.

'I just thought,' I said, a little breathless, 'a few minutes' rest might be nice for you, Mr Riversmith.'

Although he in no way showed it, I believe he may possibly have appreciated that. I believe his vanity may have been flattered. He slowed his stride, and we stepped together into the bright sunlight of the Campo. The others were seated round an outside table beneath a striped blue and white awning. To my horror, Quinty and the maid were there also. Quinty was boring the General with details of the Tour de France.

'I see Jean-François has taken the Yellow,' he was saying as we approached them, and the old man nodded agreeably. He showed me a book of flowers he'd bought, the text in Italian but with meticulously detailed illustrations of azaleas. 'Mollis and Knaphill,' he said, a forefinger following the outline of the species. 'Kurume and Glenn Dale. We shall *make* them grow.'

Otmar and Aimée were looking through their postcards. Rosa Crevelli had opened a powder compact and was applying lipstick. Having given up his effort to interest the General in bicycle-racing, Quinty was smiling his lopsided smile, his head on one side, admiring her.

'I've bought a really gorgeous hen,' I said.

I carefully unwrapped my prize. Aimée gasped when the pretty thing emerged from its black tissue paper.

'They have crocodiles and serpents as well, Aimée, but I thought the hen the best.'

'Wow, it's fantastic!'

'"Who'll help me grind my corn?" D'you know about the little red hen, Aimée?'

She shook her head.

'"I won't," said the dog. "I won't," said the cat.' I told the tale in full, as Mrs Trice had related it to me so very long ago, when I was younger than Aimée.

'Well, I never heard that one,' Quinty said. '*Capisci?*' he asked Rosa Crevelli. 'Signora's on about a farmyard fowl. *Una gallina*.'

I leaned toward Mr Riversmith, next to whom I was seated, and said I had hoped Quinty and the girl would have lunch on their own. 'I must apologize for your having to sit down with servants.'

He shook his head as if to say it didn't matter. But it *did* matter. It was presumptuous and distressing. I attracted a waiter's attention and indicated that Mr Riversmith would be grateful for an Old Fashioned and that I'd like a gin and tonic myself. I did so quietly; but Quinty has an ear for everything.

'G and t!' he shouted down the table at the waiter, who repeated the abbreviation, appearing to be amused by it. 'You like g.t.?' he offered everyone in turn. 'I like,' Rosa Crevelli said. Mr Riversmith said he didn't want an Old Fashioned.

'It wasn't arranged, she invited herself. They're lame ducks, as you might say.'

Quinty had been down and out, I went on; the girl was of gypsy stock. As I spoke, the waiter returned with my gin and tonic, and one for Rosa Crevelli as well. '*Due* g.t.!' he shouted, affecting to find the whole episode comic. When taking our orders for lunch he clowned about, striking attitudes and rolling his eyes. All this had been started off by Quinty and the maid. I drew Mr Riversmith's attention to the fact, but added that they meant no harm.

'It can be hurtful,' I said, 'but there you are.'

The General had put his horticultural manual aside and was describing to Otmar the purpose of different kinds of spades. Quinty joined in the conversation, saying something about a local firm that would supply fertilizer at a good price. When labour was required he advised the General to get estimates. In Italy nothing was done without an estimate. There was a babble of Italian from Rosa Crevelli and everyone had to wait while it was translated. It didn't amount to much, something to do with where urns for the azaleas might be obtained.

'A most extraordinary thing,' I remarked to Mr Riversmith, unable any longer to resist telling him about the dream. While I was speaking the waiter came with bottles of wine and mineral water. He joked again, pouring me two glasses of wine and then, in mock confusion, a third one. Aimée enjoyed his nonsense, and I suppose it was innocent enough.

'No more than a boy you were,' I said. 'Fifteen or so.'

But Mr Riversmith displayed no interest. I asked him if he had dreamed himself the night before and he insisted he hadn't. He rarely did, he said.

I suggested, though diffidently, that none of us can get through a night's sleep without the assistance of dreams. Sometimes we forget we dream. We remember briefly and then forget. Or do not remember at all.

'I am not familiar with the subject,' Mr Riversmith said.

Hoping to encourage him, I carefully retailed the details of the dream. I described the boy he'd been. I described the child his sister, Phyl, had been. I asked him if he remembered a Venetian blind that on occasion might have rattled, a slat tapping against the kitchen window-frame.

'No.'

The reply came too quickly. To remember, it is necessary to think for a moment, even for several minutes. But I didn't want to press any of this. I finished my drink and pushed away a plate of soup, not caring for the taste of it. It was disappointing that Mr Riversmith wasn't going to bother, but of course it couldn't be helped.

'I just thought I'd mention it,' I said.

I don't think he spoke again while we had lunch but afterwards, as we walked through the streets to where the car was, I noticed to my surprise that he attempted to engage Rosa Crevelli in conversation. Since her English scarcely exists, it must have been an extremely frustrating experience for him. It was all the more bewildering that he appeared to persevere.

I was a little upset by this and somewhat gloomily walked with the General, whose slow pace suited me. The day before I'd noticed further letters from the two firms of solicitors, so I raised the subject as we made our way together.

'I've written to say I am creating a garden.'

'Good for you, General!'

'I've been meaning to say, actually: you've no objection to Otmar and myself delaying our departure a while, have you?'

'Of course I haven't.'

'He's nervous to mention it to you, but he's wondering if the garden could be his way of paying for his board and lodging?'

'Of course it could be.'

'From me, it's a gift, you understand? I shall continue to pay my weekly whack.'

'That's as you like, General.'

Since we were passing various small cafés and bars I suggested that he might rest for a few minutes and have another cup of coffee. He readily agreed, and when we found somewhere agreeable I decided not to have more coffee but ordered a glass of grappa instead.

'A garden can't make up for anything.' The old man, quite suddenly, returned to the subject, perhaps feeling that this was the time to say it, now that he had me on my own for a few minutes. 'But at least it will mark our recovery in your house.'

'Stay as long as you like.' I replied softly, knowing that that, really, was what we were talking about.

'You're kind,' he said.

We made a detour on our journey back to my house, turning off the main road and winding our way up to a Benedictine monastery. It was cool and leafy, with a coloured sculpture high up in an archway, and another in the same position on the other side: this is the abbey of Monte Oliveto Maggiore, as close to heaven on earth as you will ever find. With the exception of the General, we all descended several flights of steps, through a forest of trees, to the monks' church in a cool hollow below. Along the cloisters were murals of St Benedict's life. Doves cooed at one another, occasionally breaking into flight. In the monks' shop mementoes were laid out tastefully.

'Gosh!' Aimée exclaimed, as delighted as she'd been by the picture of the shepherds and by the hen I'd bought. 'Otmar, isn't it fantastic?'

Otmar was always there, unobtrusively behind her. His devotion was remarkable, and constantly she turned to him, to share a detail that had caught her imagination or to tell him something she'd thought of, or just to smile.

'It is fantastic,' he said.

'What's "fantastic" in German, Otmar?'

'*Phantastisch.*'

'*Phantastisch.*'

'That is good, Aimée.'

'Would a German understand me?'

'*Ja. Ja.*'

'Tell me another word. Tell me the name of a bird.'

'*Taube* is for dove. *Möwe* is for seagull.'

'How do you say "beautiful"?'

'*Schön* is for beautiful.'

'*Schön.*'

'That is good.'

'*Möwe.*'

'That is good too.'

Mr Riversmith bought her a little red and green box with drawers in it, and then we climbed back to where the General awaited us. He had found a tea-room and was reading about flowers again.

'It's really beautiful down there,' Aimée told him. 'A monk patted my head.'

As we moved towards the car I managed to draw Otmar aside, to reassure him that his proposal for paying what was owing was quite acceptable, and to repeat that he, too, was welcome to remain in my house for as long as he wished.

'I have no skills for the work. I bring no knowledge.'

I reassured him on this point also, and for some reason as I did so a vivid picture came into my mind: of his buying the railway tickets to Milan on 5 May and counting the notes he received in change. 'Shall we have a cappuccino?' Madeleine suggested. 'There's time.' I might have placed a hand on the shoulder from which his arm had been cut away, but somehow I could not bring myself to do so. I might have said he must not blame himself. Without knowing anything, I might have said it was all right.

'It is possible,' I said instead. 'A life you did not think of when you lay in that hospital is possible, Otmar.'

For a second the eyes behind the large spectacles fearfully met mine. I remembered his fingers interlaced with Madeleine's, and the old man as straight as a ramrod beside his daughter. I remembered the two children arguing in whispers, and a workman with a shovel, standing by the railway line.

'She is going back to America,' Otmar said, and there our conversation ended.

In the car Quinty regaled Mr Riversmith with information

he'd picked up somewhere about St Mary of Egypt. 'Singer and actress she used to be,' his voice drifted back to where I was sitting, and he went on about how scavenging dogs wouldn't touch the remains of St Bibiana, and how the Blessed Lucy endured a loss of blood through her stigmata every Wednesday and Friday for three years. I was unable to hear how Mr Riversmith responded and didn't particularly try to, because that Quinty was having a field day didn't matter any more. What mattered was that Mr Riversmith was an ambitious man: that hadn't occurred to me before. He was ambitious and Francine was ambitious for him, and for herself. There were other professors with microscopes, watching other colonies of ants in other trees. He and Francine had to keep ahead. They had to get there first. What time could they devote to a child who had so tiresomely come out of the blue? Would serious ambition be interrupted in Virginsville, Pennsylvania? That's what I wondered as Quinty continued to be silly and Mr Riversmith, poor man, was obliged to listen.

When we returned I lay down for an hour; it was almost seven when I appeared downstairs again. Aimée was in bed, the General said, and wished to say good-night to her uncle and myself. He and I went together to her room, where the shutters had been latched to create an evening twilight. When Mr Riversmith spoke her name she answered at once. I sat on the edge of the bed. He stood.

'Aimée, I would like you to have the hen I bought. It's a present for you.'

To my surprise, she seemed bewildered. Her face puckered, as if what I'd said made no sense. Then she turned to her uncle.

'I didn't ever know there was a quarrel.'

'It wasn't important.'

'But it *happened*.'

'Yes, it happened.'

Since that seemed inadequate, I added:

'Disagreements don't much matter, Aimée.' And deliberately changing the subject, I added: 'Remember the picture of the shepherds?'

'Shepherds?'

'The shepherds with their dog.'

'And a *hen*?'

'No, no. The hen was what I bought for you.'

'What else was in the picture?'

'Well, sheep in a pen.'

'What else?'

'There were hills and houses,' Mr Riversmith said, and although I wasn't looking at him I guessed that that familiar frown was gathering on his brow.

'And eight trees,' I added. 'Don't you remember, we counted them?'

Through the gloom I watched her shaking her head. Her uncle said:

'I guess you remember the angel in the sky, Aimée?'

'Have you come to say good-night? I'm sleepy now.'

I mentioned the visit to the monastery, but the entire day except for that reference to a quarrel appeared to have been erased from Aimée's memory. Her breathing deepened while we remained with her. I could tell she was asleep.

'This isn't good,' her uncle said.

Of course the man was upset; in the circumstances anyone would be. He asked if he might telephone Dr Innocenti, and did so from the hall. I listened on the extension in my private room, feeling the matter concerned me.

'Yes, there will be this,' Dr Innocenti said.

'The child's suffering from periodic amnesia, doctor.'

'So might you be, signore, if you had experienced what your niece has.'

'But this came on so suddenly. Was it the excitement today, the visit to Siena?'

'I would not say so, signore.'

Mr Riversmith said he had arranged to return to Pennsylvania with Aimée in four days' time. He wondered if he'd been hasty. He wondered if his niece should be taken back to the hospital for observation.

'The journey will not harm your niece, signore.'

'All day she seemed fine.'

'I can assure you, signore, she has recovered more of herself than we once had hopes of in the hospital. What remains must be left to passing time. And perhaps a little to good fortune. Do not be melancholy, signore.'

Naturally, in all honesty, Dr Innocenti had had to say that the journey would not be harmful. It was not the journey we had to dwell upon but the destination. And this was not something Dr Innocenti could presume to mention. There were further reassurances, but clearly Mr Riversmith remained far from relieved. No sooner had the conversation with Dr Innocenti come to an end than he made a call to his wife in Virginsville. I guessed he would, and again picked up the receiver in my room. She was not surprised, the woman said. In a case like this nothing could be expected to be straightforward. Her voice was hoarse, deep as a man's, and because I'd heard it I at last pictured without difficulty the woman to whom it belonged: a skinny, weather-beaten face, myopic eyes beneath a lank fringe, eyebrows left unplucked.

'What you need's a good stiff drink,' I said a little later, when Mr Riversmith appeared in the *salotto*. He looked shaken. For all I knew, she'd given him gip after I'd put the receiver down. For all I knew, this weather-beaten woman blamed him for the mess they'd got into – having to give a home to a child who by the sound of things was as nutty as a fruitcake. Added to which, the heat in Siena might well have adversely affected the poor man's jet-lag. I poured him some whisky, since whisky's best for shock.

10

After I'd had my bath that evening I happened to catch a glimpse of myself, as yet unclothed, in my long bedroom mirror. My skin was still mottled from the warm water, the wounds of 5 May healed into vivid scars. A dark splotch of stomach hair emphasized the fleshiness that was everywhere repeated – in cheeks and thighs, breasts, arms and shoulders. To tell you the truth, I think it suits me particularly well in my middle age. I'd feel uneasy scrawny.

I chose that evening a yellow and jade outfit, a pattern of ferns on a pale, cool ground. I added jewellery – simple gold discs as earrings, necklace to match, rings and a bangle. Not hurrying, I made my face up, and applied fresh varnish to my fingernails. My shoes, high-heeled and strapped, matched the jade of my dress.

'You're putting us to shame tonight,' the General remarked as we sat to dinner on the terrace, and you could see that Otmar was impressed as well. But Mr Riversmith reacted in no way whatsoever. All during dinner you could tell that he was worried about the child.

'You mustn't be,' I said when we were alone. A local man who hired machines for ploughing had arrived, and the General and Otmar had gone to talk to him at the back of the house.

'She's suffering from a form of amnesia,' Mr Riversmith said. 'She draws the pictures and then forgets she's done them. She's forgotten a whole day.'

'We're lucky to have Dr Innocenti here.'

'Why did the German say he'd drawn the pictures?'

'I suppose because there must be an explanation for the pictures' existence. It would be worrying for Aimée otherwise.'

'It isn't true. It causes a confusion.'

Because of his distress he was as forthcoming as he'd been when he'd felt guilty about his sister. Distress brings talk with it. I've noticed that. In fairness you couldn't have called him ambitious now.

'Look at it this way, Mr Riversmith: an event such as we've shared draws people together. It could be that survivors understand one another.'

His dark brows came closer together, his lips pursed, then tightened and then relaxed. I watched him thinking about what I'd said. He neither nodded nor shook his head, and it was then that it occurred to me he bore a very faint resemblance to Joseph Cotten. I didn't remark on it, but made the point that all four of us would not, ordinarily, have discovered a common ground.

'D'you happen to know if they've given up on the case?' he asked, not responding to what I'd said.

I didn't know the answer to this question. Since the detectives had ceased to come to my house we'd been a little out of touch with that side of things. The last I'd heard was that they considered their best hope to be the establishing of a connection between the events of 5 May and some other outrage, even one that hadn't yet occurred. I repeated all that, and Mr Riversmith drily observed:

'As detective-work goes, I guess that's hardly reassuring.'

I sipped my drink, not saying anything. It was Joseph Cotten's style, rather than a resemblance. A pipe would not have seemed amiss, clenched between his strong-seeming teeth. You didn't often see those teeth because he so rarely smiled. Increasingly that seemed a pity.

'There are mysteries in this world,' I said as lightly as I could. 'There are mysteries that are beyond the realm of detectives.'

He didn't deny that, but he didn't agree either. If he'd had a pipe he would have relit it now. He would have pressed the tobacco into the cherrywood bowl and drawn on it to make it glow again. I was sorry he was troubled, even though it made it easier to converse with him. Around us the fireflies were beginning.

'I've been trying to get to know you, Mr Riversmith.'

Perhaps it was a trick of the twilight but for a moment I thought I saw his face crinkling, and the bright flash of his healthy teeth. I tapped out a cigarette from a packet of MS and held the packet toward him. He hadn't smoked so far and he didn't now. I asked him if he minded the smell of a cigarette.

'Go right ahead.'

'You brought up mysteries, Mr Riversmith.' I went on to tell him about the feeling I continued to experience – of a story developing around us, of small, daily details apparently imbued with a significance that was as yet mysterious. I spoke of pieces of a jigsaw jumbled together on a table, hoping to make him see that higgledy-piggledy mass of jagged shapes.

'I don't entirely grasp this,' he said.

'Survival's a complicated business.'

From the back of the house the voice of the Italian with the motorized ploughs came to us, a halting line or two of broken English, and then the General's reply. As soon as possible, the old man urged. It would do no harm to turn the earth over several times, now and in the autumn and the spring. The Italian said there would have to be a water line, a trench dug for a pipe from the well. There would be enough stone in the ruined stables, no need to have more cut. Dates were mentioned, argued about, and then agreed.

'It's been a long day.'

As he spoke, Mr Riversmith stood up. I begged him, just for a moment longer, to remain. I poured a little wine into his glass, and a little into mine. Because of his American background, I told him how I'd found myself in Idaho. I mentioned my childhood fascination with the Old West, first encountered in the Gaiety Cinema. I even mentioned Claire Trevor and Marlene Dietrich.

'Idaho is hardly the Wild West.'

'I was misled. I was no more than a foolish child.'

I told him how Ernie Chubbs had been going to Idaho in search of orders for sanitary-ware and had taken me with him on expenses; I told him how he'd taken me with him to Africa and then had disappeared. In the Café Rose they said they expected I'd met Mrs Chubbs, and it was clear what they were hinting at. 'A healthy woman,' they used to say. 'Chubbs's wife was always healthy.' All I knew myself was that every time Ernie Chubbs referred to his wife he had to cough.

I described Ernie Chubbs because it was relevant, his glasses, and tidy black hair kept down with scented oil. I explained that he didn't travel with the sanitary-ware itself, just brochures full of photographs. In order to illustrate a point, I was obliged to refer again to the Café Rose, explaining that he took an order there but when the thing arrived eight or so months later it had a crack in it. 'The place was unfortunate in that respect. "I Speak Your Weight", a weighing-machine said in the general toilet, but when you put your coin in nothing happened. Chubbs sold them that too. He used to be in weighing-machines.'

'I see.'

There was another line Chubbs had, what he called the 'joke flush'. When you pulled the chain, a voice called out, 'Ha! ha!' You kept pulling it and it kept saying, 'Ha! ha!' What was meant to happen was you'd give up in desperation;

then you'd open the door to go out and the thing would flush on its own. But what actually happened was that when people installed the joke flush the voice said, 'Ha! ha!' and they couldn't make it stop, and the flush didn't work no matter what they did. Another thing was, when the light was turned on in the toilet, music was meant to play but it hardly ever did.

'In the end the defective goods people caught up with Ernie Chubbs.'

'I really think I must get along to bed now.'

Women were Ernie Chubbs's weakness: he was Aries on the cusp with Taurus, a very mixed-up region for a man of his sensual disposition. Before my time he took someone else round with him on expenses, but when she wanted to marry him he couldn't afford to because of the alimony. It was then that Mrs Chubbs conveniently turned up her toes, and after that the other lady wouldn't touch him with a pole. Maybe she got scared, I wouldn't know. I was eighteen years old when I first met Ernie Chubbs, green as a pea. 'All very different from your ants,' I said.

The engine of a motor-car started. '*Buonanotte!*' the old man called out, and then Otmar wished their visitor good-night also. There was a flash of headlights as the car turned on the gravel before it was driven off.

Again Mr Riversmith stood up and this time I did so too. I led him from the terrace into the house, and to my private room. I switched the desk-light on and pointed at my titles in the glass-faced bookcase. I watched him perusing them, bending slightly.

'You're an author, Mrs Delahunty?'

I explained that the collected works of Shakespeare had been part of the furniture at the Café Rose, together with the collected works of Alfred Lord Tennyson. That was my education when it came to writing English. I knew 'The Lady of

Shalott' by heart, and the part of Lady Macbeth and 'Shall I compare thee to a summer's day?' I said:

'You might like to call me Emily.'

There was something about his forehead that I liked. And to tell the truth I liked the way, so unaffectedly, he'd said he didn't grasp what I was endeavouring to relate to him. There was reassurance in his sombre coolness. He kept coming and going, emerging when he was troubled, hiding because of nerviness when he wasn't. Clever men probably always need drawing out.

'You're Capricorn,' I said, making yet another effort to put him at ease. 'The moment I heard your voice on the phone I guessed Capricorn.'

He turned the first few pages of *Bloom of Love*. There was a flicker of astonishment in the eyes that had been so expressionlessly opaque a moment before. He picked up *Waltz Me to Paradise*, then returned both volumes to where he'd taken them from.

'Most interesting,' he said.

'Your ants are interesting too, Tom.'

Perhaps it was ridiculous to think that a professor of entomology in his middle years would ask if he might take *Little Bonny Maye* or *Two on a Sunbeam* to bed with him, but even so it was a disappointment when he didn't. We stood without saying anything for a moment, listening to the sound of one another's breathing. I kept seeing his ants, running all over the place, a few carrying others on their backs, all of them intent upon some business or other.

'I would listen if you told me, Tom. About your ants.'

He shook his head. His research was of academic interest only, and was complex. An explanation of it did not belong in everyday conversation.

'What was it you didn't grasp, Tom?'

'What?'

I smiled encouragingly, wanting to say that if he smiled more himself everything would be easier for both of us, that it was a pity to possess such strong teeth and not ever to display them. I asked him to pick out *Precious September*. By Janine Ann Johns, I said, and watched him while he did so.

'Open it, Tom.'

I asked him to look for Lady Daysmith, and to read me a single sentence concerning her. There was an initial hesitation, a shifting of the jaw, the familiar tightening of the lips. I sensed a reminder to himself of the care, and love, that had so cosseted his sister's child in this house.

'Lady Daysmith knelt,' he read eventually. *'She closed her eyes and her whisper was heard in the empty room, beseeching mercy.'*

He replaced the volume on its shelf and closed the glass-paned door on it.

'Sit down, Tom. Have a glass of grappa with me.'

He rejected this, but I begged him and in the end he did as I wished because I said it was important. I poured us each a glass of grappa. I said:

'Lady Daysmith had her origins in a Sunday-school teacher.' I described the humility of Miss Alzapiedi, her gangling height, the hair that should have been her crowning glory. 'Flat as a table up front. I turned her into an attractive woman, Tom.'

'I see.'

'All her life she never wore stockings. Her skirts came down to her shoes.'

He began to rise, his drink untouched.

'Drink your grappa, Tom. I've poured it for you.'

He sipped a little. I told him that that was how it was done: you turned Miss Alzapiedi into elegant Lady Daysmith. I told him how Miss Alzapiedi had come to my assistance when I mixed up God with Joseph. I didn't claim that making her Lady Daysmith was a reward. It was just something that had occurred.

'But it's nice, Tom. And it's nice that an old man who's had the stuffing knocked out of him can still find his last reserves in order to create an English garden in the heat of Umbria.'

'Yes, indeed.'

Illusion came into it, of course it did. Illusion and mystery and pretence: dismiss that trinity of wonders and what's left, after all? A stick of an old creature in misery as he walks up and down a hospital corridor with a holy statue in it. The suffering in the heart of a Sunday-school teacher who wears her dresses long. Dismiss it and you're face to face with a violent salesman of sanitary-ware, free-wheeling about with young girls on expenses. Dismiss the conventions of my house in Umbria and Quinty, for one, would be back where he started.

'If I gave Quinty his marching orders, Tom, he'd take his gypsy with him and they'd end up on a wasteland. They'd make a shack out of flattened oil-drums. They'd thieve from people on the streets.'

'Mrs Delahunty – '

'I've seen the tourists here looking askance at Quinty, and who on earth can blame them? You must have thought you'd come to a madhouse when he began his talk about holy women. Yet eccentric conversation's better than being a near criminal. Or so I'd have thought.'

Politely he said he found Quinty not uninteresting on the subject of hagiology. I smiled at him: once again he was doing his best. I remembered him walking beside Rosa Crevelli after we'd had lunch, making an effort to converse with her. He'd had a glass or two of wine, and I wondered if he'd thought to himself that she had an easy look to her. No reason why a reticent man shouldn't have a fancy, shouldn't go for that sallow skin and gypsy eyes, a different ball-game from Francine. But this wasn't the time to wonder for long about any of that.

Perhaps in the morning, I suggested, we might look for a bark-ant together so that he could show me his side of things, since I'd been going on so about my own. For a start, I'd no idea if a bark-ant looked different from the kind of ant that lives beneath a stone. I asked him about that, pouring just a thimbleful more grappa into my glass. I said it was fascinating what he'd said about bark-ants behaving like human beings. I asked him how they came by their name. He didn't answer, and when I looked up I discovered he was no longer in the room.

11

The old man showed me what he intended, passing on to me the gist of the deliberations that had taken place the evening before, how the Italian had pointed out that in order to create the different levels a mechanical digger rather than a ploughing machine was necessary. This, too, he could supply and operate himself. The General showed me where the terracing and the flights of steps would be. Part of the garden would be walled: the Italian had machinery for demolishing the half-ruined stables and moving the stone to where it could be attractively put to use.

The General repeated that the garden was a gift. But he did not feel he could make such drastic alterations without my agreement. He showed me where a fountain would be, and where the shade trees would be planted.

'It'll be beautiful, General.'

'A garden should have little gardens tucked away inside it. It should have alcoves and secret places, and paths that make you want to take them even though they don't lead anywhere. What grows well, you cherish. What doesn't, you throw out.'

The digger would bite into the slope beside the sunflower field. As well as terraces, there would be sunken areas. The Italian who'd come was a man of imagination; he'd entered into the spirit of the challenge. A separate well for the garden might be necessary, rather than the pipeline he'd first suggested. The old cypress tree beside the stables would remain.

'This'll be costly, General. Are you sure – '

'Yes, I'm sure.'

Then, for the last time in my presence, the old man mentioned his daughter. We stood among the rank growth of that wasted area, to which the dilapidated old buildings and rusty wheels and axles lent a dismal air. The General stared down at the ground of which he expected so much. In his daughter's lifetime he had resented the fact that what wealth he left behind would be shared with her husband. 'I would happily give all the days remaining to me if it might be now,' he murmured, and said no more.

So it was left. I had accepted gifts from men before, but never one like this, and never without strings that tied some grisly package. I was moved afresh by what was happening, by faith being kept in so many directions at once, by frailty turned into strength. The timbers of these useless buildings and the discoloured iron that had sunk into the ground would be scooped away, the fallen walls given an unexpected lease of life; an old man's dream would spread on the hill beside the sunflower slope. He knew, as I did, that he would not live to see his garden's heyday. But he knew it didn't matter.

That day was hotter, even, than the days that had preceded it. At half-past ten Aimée and her uncle went for a walk, advised to do so before the day became oppressive. There is a selection of straw hats in the outer hall, kept for the tourists, since people who come here always want to walk about the hillsides no matter what the temperature. I insisted that Aimée should wear one, and her uncle also; I warned them to keep to the roads and tracks for fear of snakes. For a few moments I watched their slow progress through the clumps of broom and laburnum, Aimée in a light-blue dress, her wide-brimmed panama too big for her, he in shirtsleeves and fawn cotton trousers, and a hat with a brown band. When they passed from sight I hurried into the house and made my way to his bedroom.

I'd hoped to find a photograph of Francine that would confirm the picture I had formed, but there wasn't one. His clothes hung neatly in the simple wardrobe, a tie was draped over the back of a chair. A sponge-bag contained an electric razor, toothbrush and toothpaste, aspirin and deodorant. Airline tickets and cufflinks were on the dressing-table; soiled laundry had been folded and placed at the bottom of one of the black Mandarina Duck bags. On the bedside table there was a grey-jacketed volume entitled *The Case for Differentia.* I opened it, but could not understand a word. Convoluted sentences trailed sluggishly down the page. Words were brandished threateningly, and repeated for good measure: *empirical, behavioural, delimit, cognitive, validation, determinism, re-endorsement. Can this be designated an urban environment?* a question posed, followed by the statement that *a quarter of the 'given population' are first-generation immigrants.* From what I could gather these were ants, not human beings. I closed the volume hastily.

Beneath it there was a blue notebook full of jottings in what I took to be the handwriting of Mr Riversmith. The script was more than a little difficult to read, pinched and without any attempt at an attractive effect. *?Is evidence, co-operation economic activities, exchange goods, service. ?Trade, familial lines. Pilsfer's recreation theory shaky. Recurrent exchange gifts cannot be taken recreational. ?Sanctions on miscreant. No evidence Pilsfer's sleep motive. Seasonal migration dubious. No evidence P's hospital theory. This surely invalid.*

I turned the pages. There were diagrams that looked like family trees without names, but with all the lines joined together, suggesting an electrical circuit of unusual elaboration and complexity. There were further references to recreation and to Pilsfer, who didn't at all appear to know what he was up to. A particular observation caught my eye, since it was heavily underscored. *Maeslink's theory exploded, premises no validity now: 3 April '87. Impossible extrapolate. By its nature, sensation indefinable.* The last entry, marked *Italy July '87,* was: *Sleeping-bag theory ignores monoist structure.* In what I'd read the word *theory* occurred four times.

All this was what occupied him. All this was what fuelled his ambition. All this was what made him reticent. I knew a man once who was scarcely able to address a word to anyone, but that reserve was as brittle as the ice it seemed like, and when it cracked there was a flow I couldn't stop: there was little evidence to suggest that Mr Riversmith was like that, even if he *was* more voluble when upset. He was eminent and distinguished and looked up to. There were people who would listen, intrigued, when he explained the world in terms of ants who bred in bark: you could tell all that by his manner. He was not aware of ordinary matters, as the Italian who was bulldozing out my garden was; in fact, he had so far displayed no signs of awareness whatsoever. His cleverness was there as a substitute and it could hardly be worthless. That's what I thought as I left his room that morning, 24 July 1987, a date I have never forgotten.

I have not forgotten it because what happened on the afternoon of that day was that I received one of the most unpleasant shocks of my life. Mr Riversmith asked permission to make yet another telephone call to Pennsylvania; I said of course, and went to my room. He was remarking, when I lifted the receiver, that he had never before encountered a romantic novelist. Then, distressing me considerably, he referred to as 'trash' what last night he had called most interesting. He referred to the grappa we'd enjoyed together as an unpleasant drink. The word 'grotesque' was used in a sentence I couldn't catch. The brief, and private, revelations I had made – in particular the death of Mrs Chubbs – were described as 'a drunken fantasy'. He said I'd gone to Idaho thinking I'd find the Wild West there, which had he listened he would have realized wasn't so. 'Some honey!' the hoarse voice at the other end more than once interrupted.

I couldn't understand it. In good faith I'd shown him my titles. I'd gone to a great deal of trouble to arrange an outing to Siena. I'd given him drink after drink and had not even considered entering them in Quinty's book. 'Her imagination has consumed her,' he said. From his tone, he could have been referring to an ant.

I replaced the receiver and simply sat there, feeling weak, as though I had been bludgeoned. He hadn't even become familiar with the books' contents: all he had done was to read a few lines because I asked him to, and to glance at the illustrations on the jackets. I smoked, and drank a little, hardly anything really. Quinty knocked on my door and said there was tea downstairs; I thanked him but did not go down. He knocked again at dinner-time, but again I chose to remain on my own. I watched the dusk gathering and welcomed it, and welcomed darkness even more. When I slept I dreamed a terrible dream:

It was Otmar who brought the thing on to the train. Long before they'd met in the supermarket he and his friends had picked the girl out. They knew all about her. She was suitable for their purpose.

In my dream I saw Otmar as a child, in the dining-room with his mother and father, Schweinsbrust on the table. There is a sudden crash, the battering down of the outside door; then four men enter the dining-room and greet the diners softly. The tears of Otmar's mother drop on to the meat and potatoes and little stewed tomatoes. His father stands up; he knows his time has come. For a moment the only sound is the ticking of the clock on the mantelpiece, between the two bronze horsemen. Otmar's mother does not cry out; she does not attempt to fling herself between the men and their prisoner. A long time ago she endeavoured to accept her husband's fate in anticipation; she, too, knew the men would one day come.

For crimes committed in Hitler's war he is the four men's prey, and the clock still ticks when they have taken him away. It ticks even though there will be no trial; the execution will be discreet. It ticks as sportingly as ever, while the tears of Otmar's mother fall on to the little stewed tomatoes, while she decides she does not wish to live herself. It ticks when she stands up and goes away, and when Otmar finds her, tied up to a light fixture in another room.

'Otmar it is,' an unhurried voice states, the children of the fathers locked in another turn of the wheel, a fresh fraternity of vengeance. Broken matchsticks are cast as lots. 'Otmar is the chosen one.'

In Carrozza 219 he strokes her arm. She'll carry the vengeance through Linata Airport, on to the plane that's bound for Tel Aviv. The victim, as Otmar's father was, is occupied now with other matters; the past is past. In the fields the sunflowers are brilliant against the pale sky. Is it Madeleine's hand that is like an ornament in the air, the same hand that dislodged the stack of mustard jars?

When I pushed the shutters back from my window the next morning the first person I saw was Mr Riversmith. He was bending over a tiny apricot shoot I knew well, no more than five inches of growth, which Signora Bardini had marked with a bamboo cane. Signora Bardini suspected it had sprouted from a stone of the fruit, either thrown down or possibly dropped by a large bird. Clover rather than grass thrived in this area at the side of my house. Two circular beds had been dug by Signora Bardini, but nothing grew in them. Only the day before the General had noticed these beds and said he intended to plant roses in them.

Although it was early I poured myself a little something on my way through the *salotto*. I sat down for a moment, bracing myself. The memory of the telephone conversation was sharper than ever in my consciousness. I wanted to dull it just a little before I spoke, again, to Mr Riversmith. I poured myself a second glass, mostly tonic really, and felt much better when I'd drunk it. I lit a cigarette and put on my sunglasses.

Mr Riversmith had moved from the apricot shoot when I reached him, and was shading his eyes with a hand in order to admire the view of the hills. Naturally I wanted to say I'd been hurt by what had been said. I wanted to refer to it in order to clear the air immediately. I felt that, somehow, there might have been an explanation. But I knew it was far better to wait.

'What a lovely morning, Mr Riversmith!'

'Yes, indeed, it is.'

'I love this time of day.'

He nodded so pleasantly in agreement that I wondered if I could possibly have misheard a thing or two on the telephone. It sometimes isn't easy when you can't see a person's face. But his face was there now, and it seemed more disarming than I remembered it, certainly more relaxed than it had been in my private room. Perhaps he had indeed been suffering from jet-lag and was now recovered. I said what I had planned to say.

'I'm afraid I was a nuisance to you when we talked on the terrace two evenings ago, Mr Riversmith.'

'No, not at all.'

'When I'm nervous I have a way of going round in circles. I'm sorry, it must have been disagreeable for you.'

He shook his head. I didn't speak at once in case he wished to comment. When he didn't I said:

'Jet-lag can be horrid.'

'Jet-lag?'

We had moved a little further away from the apricot shoot by now.

'They keep searching for a pill to take, but I believe they haven't had much success.'

He indicated his understanding by slightly inclining his head. He did not speak, and I permitted the silence to lengthen before I did so again myself.

'You were tired and I delayed you. I offended you by presuming to address you by your Christian name. I'm truly sorry.'

'It's perfectly all right.'

'You were not offended?'

'No.'

'It's friendlier to call you Tom.'

'By all means do so.'

'Professor makes you sound ancient.'

It had occurred to me that in spite of his protests to the contrary on his first evening in my house, he might have been offended that this title was never used. I said the apricot plant had grown from a stone, dropped possibly by a bird, and again wanted to mention the telephone conversation. I wanted to get it out of the way, to be told I had misheard and then to leave the subject, not ever to think about it again. But I knew it was not yet the moment. I knew there would be embarrassment and awkwardness.

'Let me show you where the garden'll be,' I said instead, and led him to the back of the house. In Italy you long for lawns, I said; in Africa too. I described all that the General and Otmar and their friend the Italian intended. I pointed to where the herb beds would be. The azaleas would be dotted everywhere, in their massive urns.

'Should be impressive,' he said. Would later he say to Francine that it was all an illusion? Would he say it was trash and only wishful thinking that an old Englishman intended to make a gift of a garden? Was he wondering now if the experience on the train had taken a greater toll of me than had been at first apparent? He looked away, and I thought it might be in case his expression revealed what he was thinking.

'Let's walk a little way, shall we?'

I led him along the dusty road I was so familiar with, by slopes of olive trees and vines. Endeavouring to keep the conversation ordinary, I was about to apologize for Quinty's conversation in the car on the way back from Siena, but then I remembered I had already made an effort to do so.

'I hope you find it peaceful here,' I said.

'Yes, indeed.'

'There's an Italian expression, professor – *far niente*. D'you know it?'

'I don't speak Italian, Mrs Delahunty.'

'No more do I. *Far niente* means doing nothing. *Dolce far niente*. It's nice to do nothing.'

'*Far niente*,' he repeated.

'You'd say it about sitting in a café. As we did in Siena. Or doing as we're doing now, ambling aimlessly. Enjoying the peace.'

'I see.'

That brought another subject to an end. Nothing was said for a while: then remembering that my companion had revealed he'd been married twice, I asked something about that, whether he considered that divorce was like death in a marriage.

'As great a sadness?' I hinted.

'Yes.'

'It cut you up, Tom?'

'Yes, it was painful.'

I dragged from him the name of his first wife: Celeste Adele. Sometimes there is not the slightest difficulty in visualizing a person spoken of, perhaps because of the intonation or expression that accompanies the reference. This was so now: the woman who appeared in my mind was kittenish and petite, dark-haired, much prettier than Francine.

'When was your first wife's birthday, Tom?'

'Adele's?' He had to think. Then: 'May twenty-nine.'

I stopped. 'No wonder it didn't work out, Tom.'

'I don't imagine our break-up had to do with her birthday!'

This opinion was delivered lightly, possibly intended as a joke. If it was, it was the first time he had endeavoured to make one since his arrival in my house.

'What's Francine's birth sign, Tom?'

'I'm afraid I'm not aware of it.'

'When's her birthday?'

'August eighteen.'

'Oh, Tom!'

He frowned, appearing to be genuinely bewildered. When I explained he said:

'I'm afraid I can't accept that individual characteristics have much to do with when a person's born.'

I didn't contradict that. I didn't argue. We walked on again. In a companionable way I slipped my arm through his. The truth was that when I'd picked up the receiver and overheard that unpleasant conversation I'd already had a drink or two, though not much by any means. Sometimes things aren't as crystal clear as they might be when you've had a drink. On top of that the line to Pennsylvania had not been all that good. He'd said something about what he called a 'little-girl voice', and that, of course, might well have been a compliment. I couldn't help thinking that it was nice to have your voice likened to a young girl's. For some reason my thoughts kept harping on that, and while they did so I kept wanting to tell him about the couple in the travelling entertainment business who'd perished when their motor-cycle soared towards heaven over the top of a Wall of Death. It was ludicrous of course, but I wanted to tell him – of all people – about taking that dog for a walk by the sea, and about the person I'd assumed to be my father importuning me in a cinema and in a shed and finally in a bedroom. I even wanted to tell him about the Oleander Avenue scandal. But he was cautious himself in what he said and in time I caught caution from him.

'Was it a hell with Adele, Tom?'

'We were unsuited.'

'She left you in the end?'

'No.'

'Geminis often do the leaving. I only wondered. Did Adele have children later on?'

He replied, rather curtly, that Adele was forty-three when they parted and had not had children, though in fact she had re-married. I said I was sorry it had been a hell with her.

We paused and looked back. I pointed out a hill-town in the misty distance, and a few more landmarks, a tower that two Swedish women had begun to renovate and then had given up, a rock formation that looked like human figures. As we walked on again I said:

'Why did they dislike one another, Tom? Your sister and your wife?'

He was reluctant to supply this information. His eyes had a faraway look and I remembered the jottings in the notebook at his bedside. No doubt he was among those jottings now, no doubt castigating Pilsfer for some fresh inadequacy. I pressed him, very gently. He said:

'They didn't dislike one another. It was simply that my sister wanted me to try again with Adele.'

'But it was your life, eh?'

'She didn't seem to appreciate that it was.'

Time had passed, they hadn't made it up: there was more to all this than the bald explanation I'd been offered. Perhaps he didn't know: men sometimes don't. But I sensed that his sister had recognized Francine for what she was and made it clear to her at the time of the divorce. 'It won't last, Tom': he didn't confess his sister – less outspoken and quieter in his presence – had said that, but I guessed she had. I also guessed that the wound this opinion left behind was deep.

'There's another very good Italian word, Tom. *Colpa*.'

'What's it mean?'

Again I was careful not to alarm him. *Colpa* meant guilt, I explained. The General experienced guilt because of his daughter. Otmar experienced it because he was responsible for Madeleine's presence in Italy. 'And you quarrelled with your sister instead of standing up to Francine.'

He said something I didn't catch. We turned off the road on to a path that wound up a hill where umbrella pines grow in clumps. Here we must keep a special eye out for sleepy vipers, I warned. Better to have worn rubber boots, but Quinty's would be too small for him, and it was only after we'd begun our walk that I realized there was something on that particular hill I wanted him to see.

'This is a beautiful country, Tom. There are beautiful moments hidden away in corners. I have seen, near the Scala in Milan, a stout little opera singer practising as he strolled to a café. I have seen a wedding in the cathedral at Orvieto, when the great doors were thrown wide open and the bride and groom walked out into the sunshine. Something choked in my throat, Tom.'

I believe he nodded. Sometimes his gestures were so slight it was hard to make them out. There was the tranquillity of my house, I went on; in time there would be the garden. Where there had been only rusted iron and tumbled-down buildings before, birds would nest. Bees would search for honey among the flowers.

'It is as though, Tom, we are all inside a story that is being composed as each day passes. Does that explain it better?'

'I guess I don't entirely grasp what you're suggesting. And about my sister – '

'All right, Tom, all right.' I pressed his arm a little closer. He was on the way to becoming agitated, and really there was no need for that. Why should not Aimée be healed, I asked him, as the scratches on my face had healed already, as Otmar's stump would heal, and the General's leg?

'That is what we hope for.'

'She is happy here, you know. Or as happy as she can be at the moment.'

'My wife and I are extremely grateful to you – '

'Is there not a sacrifice you would make, Tom? After years of keeping your young sister at arm's length, through no fault of hers? Do you not owe something to her memory? As the old man does to his daughter's and Otmar to Madeleine's?'

'I've come here to bring my sister's child home.' He spoke flatly; stolidly, I thought. For the first time he sounded a little stupid, although I knew that was ridiculous. 'I am taking in my sister's child,' he said.

Again I was aware of the jottings in the notebook, the darting swiftness of a mind reflected in that impatient scribbling. He knew about the brains of ants. He knew about the nature of their energy. His own brain contained the details of their thought processes or whatever he liked to call them. Of course he could not be stupid.

'Could it be, Tom, that you had to come here to know you should go back alone?'

'Mrs Delahunty – '

'Look,' I interrupted, feeling it was necessary to do so. 'That's the grave of an American soldier.'

I pointed at an iron cross in the grass beside the path. I explained why there was no inscription.

'It is in memory of one man, but it also stands for many. The soldiers of the official enemy gave food and cigarettes to the peasants when the peasants were near starving. One man in particular gave all he had; they didn't even know his name. He died here in some pointless skirmish, but long afterwards they didn't forget him. What a gesture, Tom, to give away your food because you can go without and strangers cannot! And what a gesture, in return, to put a cross up to a nameless benefactor! It can't have been much food, or many cigarettes.'

I stepped forward when I'd finished and tore away grass and weeds from the base of the cross. Then we turned and retraced our steps. He had made no comment whatsoever on the soldier's grave. I took his arm again.

'They thought it was a miracle, Tom, that a soldier should do that. They put a cross up to a miracle.'

My sandals were covered with dust. So were his shoes. The paint on my toenails had temporarily been deprived of its gleam. Against the softness of my breast I could feel a tightening in the muscles of his arm.

'May I tell you something, Tom? Will you listen?'

'I have been listening.'

'Two men in love came to my house, dying a little more each day. In my house a son was terrified of his mother because fear was what she'd instilled in him since his birth, because she couldn't bear to let him go. In my house the women of a *ménage à trois* were cynically used. Pity made me gasp for breath, for there was no escape for any of them. It's different now, Tom.'

There had been a terrible evil was how I put it to him, but in this little corner of Italy there was, again, a miracle. No one could simply walk back into the world after the horror of Carrozza 219. Three survivors out of all the world's survivors had found a place in my house. One to another they were a source of strength. Again I referred to the garden. I quoted the lines that had come to me, only to bewilder me until the General spoke so extraordinarily of a gift.

'Dare we turn our backs on a miracle, Tom?'

I sought his fingers, the way one does when one speaks like that, but roughly he disengaged himself. Suddenly he was cross and I thought he was going to shout, as other men have in my presence. But he didn't. He simply looked at me, not saying anything at all, not speaking again, not answering questions when I asked them. I offered him a drink when we arrived back at the house, but he said he didn't want a drink at nine o'clock in the morning.

12

After that morning's walk I knew what Francine was.

Francine was a disruptive; she couldn't help herself. Francine had seen him and had desired him. Francine considered Celeste Adele a nobody, with her too-sweet manner and her looks and her bird-brain. 'I want Tom Riversmith,' Francine said aloud, although there was no one in the room except herself. 'God damn that silly bitch to hell!' Francine had lost her own husband because he'd been playing around. Fourteen years of marriage, three children conceived and born, and still he came home with someone else's smell. A girl in a panty-hose department – one o'clock in the morning, he'd confessed to that. Francine didn't ask him how he'd come across a panty-hose employee. She only wondered if it was true or if he was getting at her by making her second best to such a person. She'd stopped caring years ago.

That was why she was alone when she discovered she was on a wavelength with Tom Riversmith. Celeste Adele gave itsy little cocktail parties because she liked to play at being a hostess. She handed round Japanese crackers shaped like sea-shells; she made Tom cut slivers of lemon and use a shaker. He did his best among the real-estate people she invited, the lawyers and art-gallery people, all of them off-campus, not his type at all.

'Now *join* us,' Celeste Adele would welcome in a sugary gush as soon as you stepped into the room, where the chatter was already like a tumult. She loved noise. Later, when the party really got going, she put on Big Band music. 'Having a good time', she called it.

Francine had been taken to the first such occasion by a man who'd once invited her to the movies, and once to the Four Seasons for dinner. She knew that nothing was going to come of the relationship. Over ribs at the Four Seasons he'd talked about a wife he'd left and how he regretted that now. 'It's always a gas at the Riversmiths',' he promised, adding that Celeste Adele Riversmith loved to see new faces. On the way, driving with the radio on, he extolled the virtues of his ex-wife, so tediously that Francine moved away from him as soon as they reached their destination. 'I'm Tom Riversmith,' her host introduced himself, finding her alone.

Vaguely recognizing her from the campus, he was interested in her presence at a party of his wife's. (Later Francine learnt that Celeste Adele never invited university people to her parties because she considered it did her husband good to mix what she called 'the real world'.) Francine was working on the newly discovered Kristo papers at the time and he was fascinated: four years of Kristo's research, thought to be lost in the swamps of Cambodia, had come to light in the safe of a New York hotel.

'You're fortunate.' He sounded envious. For more than eleven years, since Kristo's death, there'd been the mystery of the missing notes, with nothing to indicate where they might possibly be. Kristo, who'd trusted no one, had been notorious for jealously guarding every detail of the evidence he turned up.

'Yes, I have been fortunate.'

She liked his reticence. She couldn't imagine him blustering like the man she'd married and had spent so long with, a campus flop if ever there was one. She couldn't imagine him lying, or being caught with a girl in the back of a sedan. He'd be grizzled when he was older – grey and grizzled, and that would suit him.

'I will always despise you for this,' his sister said when several months had passed.

She stood there, a woman Francine had never seen before, a woman who'd travelled three thousand miles to make that statement. Tom *needed* Celeste Adele, their marriage was a perfectly satisfactory one. Tom and Celeste Adele were opposites, but as often as not opposites belonged together, and they did in this case.

'You've smashed your way in,' his sister bitterly accused. 'You're taking what you can get. You're only thinking of yourself.'

There were tears then, but they weren't Francine's. They ran, unchecked, on the other woman's cheeks. Francine didn't attempt to argue.

'She's done so much for you,' his sister pleaded with Tom. 'You couldn't give her children. You used up her best years. Please, Tom, you mustn't turn around and tell her she doesn't matter.'

He shook his head. He hadn't told Adele that.

'What you're doing says it.'

She begged him, while Francine watched and listened. He'd never been like this, his sister said, and then repeated it. He'd always had a heart before.

'It's best,' he quietly muttered.

Hopelessly now, she disagreed. More spurts of tears came, but then she calmed. She blew her nose and wiped at her cheeks. Francine thought that with all this guff out of her system she'd accept the inevitable, would realize she'd gone too far and say so. There was a moment for an apology, for a mumbled effort to repair unnecessary damage. But no apology came.

'You foul bitch,' his sister snapped, like ice cracking. Then she went.

13

The old man lolled in the ladder-backed chair, Aimée was perched on one of the peacock stools. Looking down from the top of the stairs, I couldn't hear what he was murmuring but I was aware of her pleasure in his tenderness.

'I'd love to see England.' Just for a moment, Aimée's voice floated to me, and again the old man murmured.

'The last day.' Otmar had quietly joined me and was looking down also. Through the mist of my tears he seemed even more sombre than he'd been of late: a face I can only describe as defeated was turned in my direction when he spoke, as though the prospect of the child's going left him bereft. Our eyes held, and locked, and the dream I'd had about him took vivid form again. For a moment it seemed like a shaft of truth, coming to complete the story of that summer, illuminating everything. I saw the matchsticks broken, some long, some short. I watched the choice being made. 'Otmar is the chosen one,' the unhurried voice said, and I must have swayed, for he put his hand out to assist me.

At dinner that evening we were quiet. Aimée's clothes, all of which had been bought while she was in the hospital, were already packed into the bag Mr Riversmith had brought specially from America, matching the black Mandarina Duck luggage Francine had chosen for him.

The General hardly opened his mouth; nor did Otmar; nor

I, come to that. Mr Riversmith must have found it restful. He passed a remark or two and afterwards went off for a stroll on his own. I kept reminding myself that if we'd asked him he would have held forth eloquently about the digestive tracts of his chosen creature: an understanding of the human condition didn't come into it. For all I knew, he privately considered that people damaged in an outrage were best forgotten, delegated to a rubbish tip, as the broken metal and bloodstained glass had been.

I listened for his return and, when I heard him passing through the hall, I considered going to wish him good-night, but I did not feel entirely up to it. In the kitchen I poured boiling water on to a tea-bag and dropped a slice of lemon into the glass. I fished the tea-bag out immediately, just as the water changed colour. I added a measure of grappa as I always do when I take tea as late as this, for on its own it keeps me awake. I carried the glass on to the terrace. The sky was clear and full of stars. I could hear the whirring of mosquitoes, but the fireflies all had gone. It was as warm as day.

'Madeleine.' Otmar's voice echoed, repeating the girl's name, nothing more. As I sipped my tea, I heard as well the voice of Miss Alzapiedi telling us about the devil cast out of the Syrophoenician woman's daughter. When evil was made good it was as though the evil had never existed. The greatest wonder of all, Miss Alzapiedi said.

In the kitchen I threw away the remains of my tea. I arranged two glasses and the grappa bottle on a tray. I was wearing an Indian silk dressing-gown, in shades of orange, and slippers that matched it, with gold stitching. I spent a moment in my room, applying a little make-up to my lips and eyes, a little powder, and eau-de-Cologne. I ran a comb through my hair.

When I knocked softly on his door there was no answering murmur. I had hoped he might be awake, thinking about things, but clearly he wasn't. I pushed open the door and for a moment stood there, framed against the dim light of the corridor, before I moved towards his bedside table. I put the tray down and switched the light on. The notebook and the grey-jacketed volume had not yet been packed. I crossed the room again to close the door.

'Once I sold shoes, Tom.' I said that to myself, even though I spoke his name and glazed at his sleeping face. I stood leaning against the door, not immediately wishing to be closer to him or to wake him. I was still aware of the stockinged feet of women, of old shoes cast aside while I knelt and fitted whatever it was the women desired. As hot as ovens, the feet odorously perspired. 'Swollen from walking, dear. Blown up beyond their size.' They always bought shoes that were too small. The narrower fit, dear. Easily take the narrower.' They stared down at the flesh that overlapped the straps and at the little fancy buckles. 'Yes, I'd say they suit, dear.'

Quietly I moved to where he slept. His mouth was drawn down a little as if in some private despair, but I knew this was not the reason. In sleep his forehead wasn't wrinkled, his closed eyes were tranquil. The lips' expression was only a rictus of the night.

'Mr Riversmith,' I whispered. 'Mr Riversmith.'

He stirred, though only slightly, one limb or another changing position beneath the sheet that covered him. I turned away, feeling I should not be too close when he awoke in case he was alarmed. I sat on the room's single chair, half obscured by shadows in a corner.

Again my thoughts were interrupted by moments from my past. In the dining-room of the public house the clerks roughly called out their orders. In the Café Rose I opened a leathery old volume and was lost in another world: *Only reapers, reaping early, in among the bearded barley, hear a song that echoes cheerly* ... 'Two shepherd's pie 'n' chips. A toad-'n-the-hole. A plaice 'n' peas.' You had to repeat the orders so that the clerks could hear; you had to catch their attention, otherwise you'd bring the wrong plateful and then they'd jeer at you, asking you how long you'd been at it. 'Nice pair of nylons, them.' Quick as a flash the clerks would get a hand on you. On the S.S. *Hamburg* I was in love.

'Oh,' Mr Riversmith said.

'It's all right, Mr Riversmith.'

He pushed himself up, leaning on an elbow. He was looking straight at the grappa bottle. He didn't quite know what was what. My voice might have belonged to the sleep he'd come from. He didn't see me in the shadows.

'Nothing's wrong, Mr Riversmith.'

I remembered how, time and time again, I had lain there in the heat of Africa, waiting for whichever man had money that day. Afterwards, downstairs, I would make coffee and cook. The men played cards, I smoked and drank a lemonade. People who didn't exist – not the people of the books I'd found but people of my own – flitted in from somewhere: as I've said before, I'd never have written a word if I hadn't known the hell that was the Café Rose.

'What time is it?'

'Three, I think.'

'Is something – '

'No, nothing's wrong.'

I rose, smiling at him, offering further reassurance. I poured some grappa, for him and for myself. I offered him a glass.

'Look, I don't think I can drink just now.'

'Tomorrow you'll be gone. Take just a sip.'

I returned to the chair in the corner. Tomorrow they'd both be gone.

'I was fast asleep,' he said, the way people who've been roused do.

'I wanted to say I'm sorry.'

'Sorry?'

'For this morning.'

'That doesn't matter.'

'It matters to me, Mr Riversmith.'

Even now, he wasn't quite awake yet. In an effort to shake off his drowsiness he closed his eyes tightly and opened them again. He sighed, no doubt in a further effort to combat that lingering sleep.

'I was almost dreaming myself,' I confessed, 'even though no one could be more wide awake.'

He hadn't taken a sip of his grappa yet. I thought the hand that held the glass might have been shaking due to his not being properly awake; I wasn't sure.

'Phyl didn't care for Francine, and Francine is to be Aimée's second mother. That's all I'm saying, Tom.'

Still the glass was not lifted to his lips.

'You can't blame Francine for hating Phyl, Tom. If you're hated you hate back. It would be straining any woman's humanity not to.'

'My sister is dead. I'd prefer not to discuss this.'

'I was there when her death occurred, Tom,' I gently reminded him.

'My sister's child will be looked after by my wife and myself. To suggest otherwise is ridiculous.'

'I know, Tom, I know. You will take Aimée back to Pennsylvania, and Francine will make efforts – an extra cut of lemon meringue pie, another chocolate cookie. And you will say, when things get dodgy, let's go to the movies or let's drive to Colorado to see the Rockies. You'll buy Aimée a kitten; you'll make excuses for the weakness of her high-school grades; you'll say how pretty she is. But underneath it all Francine's resentment smoulders. Francine is jealous of the attention you have to lavish on your sister's child because of all that's happened. Francine tries, but your sister spoke to her like that. Why should she be reminded of it now, day after day?'

For the second time I witnessed his anger. Crossly, he said I knew nothing whatsoever about the woman he was married to and very little about him. How could I possibly predict Aimée's grades at high school?

I listened. I felt indulgent towards him, protective almost; he hadn't experienced much, he hadn't been much around; he didn't understand how one woman can guess accurately about another. At the Café Rose men had insisted that I appeared to know only too well the women they told me about. 'What must I do?' the ivory cutter demanded. 'Emily, tell me how I may have her.' But when I told him, when I was frank and explained that any woman could see it coming that his violence would land him in gaol, he turned sullen and disagreeable.

'I liked the look of Phyl, Tom.'

'What you liked or didn't like about my sister is without relevance.'

'It's just an observation. I only thought you'd care to know.'

'You saw my sister on a train. In no way whatsoever were you acquainted with her. Yet you speak as if you knew her well.'

Again I paused before responding. Then I told him about the meeting in the supermarket, the jars of mustard that had fallen when Madeleine reached for the herbs, the first cup of coffee she'd had with Otmar. I watched his face as I spoke; I watched his eyes, and was prepared to repeat what I was saying if they momentarily closed.

'There is nothing left of Otmar now. No will, no zest. Otmar's done for. That's why he will remain here.'

'I must ask you to leave me now.'

'The old man's done for too.'

'Mrs Delahunty, I know you've been through a traumatic ordeal – '

'It's unkind to call me Mrs Delahunty, Tom. It's not even my name.'

The dark brows closed in on one another. The forehead wrinkled in a frown. His tongue damped his lips, preparatory to speech, I thought. But he did not speak.

'Is there not a chance you would take, Tom? That a woman such as I can have a vision?'

'The fact that my sister's child spent some time in your house after the tragedy does not entitle you to harass me. I am grateful. My wife is grateful. The child is grateful. May I pass that message on to you, Mrs Delahunty? And may I be permitted to go back to sleep now?'

I rose from the shadows and stood above him, my replenished glass in my hand. I spoke slowly and with emphatic clarity. I said I was unable to believe that he, a man of order and precision, an ambitious man, stubborn in his search for intellectual truth where insects were concerned, refused to accept the truth that had gathered all around him.

'I don't know what you're talking about, Mrs Delahunty.'

'It frightens you, as it frightens me. For weeks the German boy was like a blob of jelly. The General would willingly have put a bullet through his head. The child went into hiding. More had occurred than a visit to a dentist, you know.'

'Why are you pestering me in this way?'

'Because you're dishonest,' I snapped at him. I hadn't meant to, and as soon as I'd spoken I apologized. But his tetchiness continued.

'You've pestered me since I arrived here. You talk to me in a way I simply fail to comprehend. I have said so, yet you persist.'

'One day the child will know about that quarrel and what

was said. One day she'll reach up and scratch Francine's eyes out.'

He made some kind of protest. I bent down, closer to him, and emphasized that this wasn't a change of subject, though it might possibly appear so. I described the scene in Otmar's boyhood: the fat congealing on the Schweinsbrust, the bronze horsemen on the mantelpiece. I told him how Otmar's father was led away, and how Otmar and his mother had listened to the dull ticking of the clock. I described the children of the fathers locked, years later, in another turn of the wheel, and Otmar choosing the shortest matchstick.

'What on earth are you talking about?'

What I'd said had caused him to sit up. His hair was slightly tousled. I told him not to be silly, to take a little grappa because he might feel the need of it. But he didn't heed me. 'What *is* this?' he persisted.

'I'm talking about what happened,' I said. 'I'm talking about people getting on to a train, and what happened next, and Quinty taking in three victims of a tragedy because they were conveniently there, because Quinty on all occasions is greedy for profit.'

'You are insinuating about the German.'

I poured myself another drink. I lit a cigarette. Before I could reply he spoke again.

'Are you suggesting the German had something to do with what occurred on the train? Has he made some kind of confession to you? Are you saying that?'

'How can we know, Tom, the heart and mind of a murderer when he wakes up among his victims? How can we know if fear or remorse is the greater when he lies helpless among the helpless? If my house is a sanctuary for Otmar it is his rack as well. Any day, any hour, the *carabinieri* may walk from their car, dropping their cigarettes carelessly on to the gravel. Any day, any hour, they may seek him in my garden. Does he choose this torment, Tom? We may never know that either.'

He was listening to me now. For the first time since he'd arrived in my house he had begun to listen to me. When I paused he said:

'What exactly are you saying?'

'I'd love it if you'd take a little grappa, Tom.'

'I don't want any grappa. Why do you keep pressing drink on me? At all hours of the day and night you seem to think I need drink. You make appalling accusations – '

'I'm only saying this might be so. Tom, no one can be certain about anything except the perpetrators – we both know that. No one but they can tell us if we're right when we guess it was a crime turned into an accident.'

'Have you or have you not grounds for making these statements about the German?'

I paused. I wanted him to be calm. I said:

'I had a dream, and when next I looked into those moist eyes behind the discs of his spectacles all of it was there. He lost his nerve. Or at the very last moment – perhaps at Orvieto railway station – he fell in love with her. In relief and happiness he stroked her arm in Carrozza 219, perhaps even whispering to himself a prayer of thanksgiving. Then came the irony: the accident occurred.'

'A *dream*?'

I explained that there was evidence, all around us, of what each and every one of us is capable of. There was the purchase of a female infant so that a man could later satisfy his base desires. A man who lavished affection on a pet could lay his vicious plans while an infant still suckled a bottle. Quinty scarred a young girl's life. In the Café Rose my flesh felt rotten with my loathing of it.

'The old man longed for unhappiness in his daughter's marriage. You rejected your young sister in favour of a predatory woman. If Otmar is guilty there is redemption in a child's forgiveness, and for Aimée a way back to herself in offering it. If Otmar is guilty the miracle may be as marvellous as the soldier giving away his food.' Ages ago it had struck me that there was something odd about Madeleine's journey. 'Flights from Rome full,' he would have lied.

'You're drunk, Mrs Delahunty. All the time I've been in your house you've been drunk. You wake me up at three o'clock in the morning with your garbled rigmaroles about executions and vengeance, expecting me to return to Pennsylvania without my niece just because you've had a dream. It's monstrous to suggest that my niece should continue to grow fond of a boy you claim might be the murderer of her family. It's preposterous to invent all this just in order to make a fantasy of the facts.'

In that same manner he went on speaking. He said it was inconceivable that an innocent girl had been stalked in the manner I described. It was inconceivable that a total stranger had caused her to fall so profoundly in love that a relationship had been formed which on his side was wholly deceitful. An incendiary device could not have been packed into her luggage without her knowledge. Such a device could not pass undetected through Linata Airport. No terrorist attack could possibly have been planned with such ineptitude. And terrorists did not go in for changes of heart.

'Please let me sleep,' he said.

Angrily I shouted at him then, all gentleness gone, not caring if I woke the household. I could feel the warmth of a flush beginning in my neck, and creeping slowly into my face.

'You're a man who always sleeps,' I snapped at him. 'You'll sleep your way to the grave, Mr Riversmith.'

I gulped at what remained of my drink and poured some more. His glass was still where he had placed it on the bedside table. I picked it up and forced it into his hand. A little of the liquid spilt on to his pyjama front. I didn't care.

'Hell is where men like you wake up, Mr Riversmith, with flames curling round their naked legs.'

He said nothing. He feared my wrath, as other men have. I calmed, and wiped the spilt drink from his pyjamas.

'You're extremely drunk,' he said.

It's always easy to maintain a person's drunk. It's an easy way for a man to turn his back. While I looked down at him in his bed a memory of the car-girls of 1950 came into my mind, I don't know why. A drizzle was falling as they sheltered in doorways, their faces yellow in the headlights of the cars. I didn't mention them because I couldn't see that they were relevant. I prayed instead that at last he would understand. 'Please, God,' I said in my mind.

I sat down on the edge of the bed and leaned in toward him, determined that he should visualize the picture I painted: the evening fireflies just beginning beyond the terrace, the General in a linen suit, Otmar among the shrubs of the garden, Aimée smiling. Survivors belonged together, no matter how eccentric it seemed. Normality had ceased for them: why should she not grow fond, and come to understand the bitterness there'd been? Why should she not?

'Don't come closer to me,' he warned unpleasantly. 'I've never given you this kind of encouragement.'

My Indian dressing-gown had accidentally parted. Hastily he looked away. I prayed that a blink of light would enter his expressionless eyes, but while I begged with mine his remained the same. I said:

'Among the few possessions that remained to Otmar after the incident I found a photograph of his mother.'

A newspaper item that told of her death was pasted to the back of it. If the pillow-talk of the Austrian ivory cutter had not always been in German I wouldn't have been able to comprehend a word. But I stumbled through it, and learnt to my astonishment that Otmar's mother had hanged herself from the electric light, exactly as in my dream.

But when I told him Mr Riversmith wasn't in the least astonished. He stared blankly back at me, even though I repeated what I'd said twice to ensure that the order of events had clearly registered. Speaking carefully and slowly, I described the scene: how I had stood among Otmar's last few belongings with the photograph in my right hand, how I had taken nearly ten minutes to comprehend the German, how I had entered the *salotto* fifteen minutes later and found Otmar and the child playing their game with torn-up pieces of paper. My dream had been a month earlier, I said.

The eyes of Thomas Riversmith didn't alter. I did not speak again.

If someone had had a camera there would be a record of the General with his hand held out and Mr Riversmith about to shake it. There would be an image of Signora Bardini still holding the sandwiches she had made for their journey, and Rosa Crevelli saying something to Quinty, and Aimée smiling up at Otmar. There would be one of me too, in a pale loose dress and sunglasses, still standing where Mr Riversmith had turned his back on me when I endeavoured to say goodbye.

I wish a photograph had been taken because just for a moment everything was of a piece and everyone was there. Ten figures stood on the gravel in front of my house, each shadowed by other people, although the camera would not have caught that subtlety. Francine was there, and Celeste Adele, and Phyl and her husband and Aimée's brother. The General's daughter, his son-in-law and his wife were there, and Madeleine, and the girl whom Quinty had wronged. All sorts were there with me.

'Mr Riversmith.' Quinty beckoned, and Mr Riversmith walked towards the car. Aimée carried the hen that was my gift to her.

The dust thrown up by the car wheels settled, and rose

again when the machines that were to make the garden came. I watched them arrive, and watched while earth was turned, in preparation for the planting in the autumn. Letters from strangers also came that morning. *I thought Oberon would never ask her. What a joyful outcome that was in the end!* Mrs Edith Lumm of Basingstoke wrote that she and her husband, staying with her husband's sister in Shropshire, had visited Mara Hall, although it was not called by that name any more. Her husband and his sister had pooh-poohed the idea that it was the house which featured in my story, but she herself was certain because of details she'd noticed, the maze for a start. Trimleigh Castle it was called now, being an hotel.

That day just happened, time ordinarily passed. It didn't require much of an effort to know that in the car Quinty chatted while Mr Riversmith considered the validity of a rule structure, and said to himself that Pilsfer had got that wrong also. On the plane the child slept, and a few notes were scrawled in the blue notebook, important thoughts put down: hierarchism was almost certainly the governing factor.

My friend wonders if Derek ever turned up again, and wonders how Rose fares in later life. My friend – Miss Jaci Rakes – believes Rose's love for Rick may not be constant. All through the afternoon the engines clanked and rattled, moving stone and earth, roughly laying out paths and flowerbeds. No one said there was something wrong because the child had gone, not Otmar certainly, not the old man.

Time was gained as it passed, hours added to Aimée's life. That evening in Virginsville the untended skin of Francine's cheek was rough to the touch in Aimée's first embrace. 'How about scrambled eggs?' Francine suggested as they drove through rain to the house. 'Will you help me make scrambled eggs, Aimée, the first thing in your new home?' The child was silent, staring at the rain on the windshield, the wipers swishing back and forth.

'You would like something?' Quinty said, coming to my private room, not knocking, for he never does. He didn't in the Café Rose and the habit stuck.

'No, I'm all right, Quinty.'

He changed my ashtray. He placed a little ice-box we have on my desk, with a lemon he had sliced. He left me a fresh glass.

'I'm all right,' I said again.

Darkness came in Pennsylvania. The Riversmiths lay beneath a sheet, his pyjamas bundled away and Francine's lean body naked also. Strength passed from one to the other, now that they were together again. Nutty as a fruitcake that child was, but they'd manage somehow. They'd think of something, being in the thinking business, both of them.

14

By now that summer belongs to the shadows of the past.

I watch the videos of old Westerns with the outside shutters of the *salotto* drawn against the afternoon light. I smoke, and sip a little tonic water livened with just a taste of spirits. The stagecoach horses neigh and judder when they're pulled up with a jerk. Masked men twitch their guns, indicating how they want the passengers to hand over their valuables. One of the men is nervous, which makes it worse. He spews out chewed tobacco. Far away and unaware, the sheriff puts his feet up.

The old man died.

Two autumns later, when Dr Innocenti visited my house for the last time it was to tell us that in Virginsville they decided that expert care was no more than the child's due. Better for her own sake to be looked after by people who were skilled, in a place that contained others of her kind.

One day I looked down into the garden and saw that Otmar had gone, into whatever oblivion he had chosen.

Except to write about that summer I have never since sat down at my black Olympia, and never shall again. I haven't learned much, only that love is different among survivors. The caravan passed by because we hesitated, but that is how things are.

The tourists come again now. They talk of Lake Trasimeno and the attractions of the hill-towns, the cafés in the sun. They visit Siena and write their postcards, they play their bridge. In my house I am the presence you are familiar with, as you can see me now. I am as women of my professional past often are, made practical through bedroom dealings, made sentimental through fear. I know all that, I do not deny it. I do not care much for the woman I am, but there you are. None of us has a choice in that.

In my garden the shrubs are parched because Quinty's search for someone to tend them is half-hearted due to his desire to save money, even though the money's mine. The tourists upbraid me and sometimes become angry, a withered petal rubbed between finger and thumb, the shreds accusingly held out. The Germans shake their heads in disapproval, the French say it's typical, the English get the hose going and water the azalea urns. I explain to them that all this, too, is how things are. They politely listen, but afterwards they frown and mutter.

Perhaps I'll become old, perhaps not. Perhaps something else will happen in my life, but I doubt it. When the season's over I walk among the shrubs myself, making the most of the colours while they last and the fountain while it flows.

FOR MORE OUTSTANDING LITERATURE FROM WILLIAM TREVOR, LOOK FOR THE

"One of the best writers of our era."
—The New York Times Book Review

Felicia's Journey
Felicia is unmarried, pregnant, and penniless. She steals away from a small Irish town and drifts through the industrial English Midlands, searching for the boyfriend who left her. Instead she meets up with Mr. Hilditch, who is looking for a new friend to join the five other girls in his Memory Lane. But the strange, sad, terrifying tricks of chance unravel both his and Felicia's delusions.

"A page-turner marked by brilliant psychological suspense."
—The Philadelphia Inquirer

"Perfectly executed and chilling . . . A sad and oddly moving tale of lost opportunities and misplaced hopes."
—Michiko Kakutani, *The New York Times*
ISBN 0-14-029021-4

The Hill Bachelors
A collection of twelve beautifully rendered tales, *The Hill Bachelors* is a stunning reflection on men and women and the heartbreak of missed opportunities.

"The poignancy of these stories is heartbreaking but never sentimental, with Trevor's ability to evoke the infinitesimal detail of interior life breathtaking enough to make one weep."
—The Baltimore Sun
ISBN 0-14-100217-4

After Rain
Another collection of twelve dazzling stories acclaimed by the *San Francisco Chronicle* as "short fiction at its finest."

"Trevor seems to have no boundaries, no limits to his powers of compassion and vision." —*Elle*

ISBN 0-14-025834-5

COMING TO PENGUIN IN THE FALL OF 2003

The Story of Lucy Gault

Shortlisted for the 2002 Man Booker Prize

The Gault family leads a life of privilege in early 1920s Ireland, but the threat of arson leads nine-year-old Lucy's parents to leave Ireland for England, her mother's home. Lucy cannot bear the thought of leaving Lahardane. On the day before they are due to leave, Lucy runs away, hoping to convince her parents to stay, but instead she sets off a series of tragic misunderstandings that affect all of the inhabitants of Lahardane and the perpetrators of the failed arson attack for the rest of their lives.

"*The Story of Lucy Gault* is one of Trevor's finest works . . . Few living writers are capable of such mournful depth, and here he has given us an evensong to time itself." —*The Boston Globe*

"Trevor has once again captured the terrible beauty of Ireland's fate, and the fate of us all—at the mercy of history, circumstance, and the vicissitudes of time." —*The Atlantic Monthly*

"Trevor's measured prose achieves such a quiet grandeur that the author of *After Rain*, *The Hill Bachelors* and *Felicia's Journey* surpasses even himself." —*The Philadelphia Inquirer*